Keys to Love

Keys to Love

DOROTHY BRENNER FRANCIS

Thorndike Press • **Chivers Press**
Waterville, Maine USA Bath, England

This Large Print edition is published by Thorndike Press, USA and by Chivers Press, England.

Published in 2002 in the U.S. by arrangement with Maureen Moran Literary Agency.

Published in 2002 in the U.K. by arrangement with the author.

U.S. Hardcover 0-7862-4036-9 (Romance Series)
U.K. Hardcover 0-7540-4863-2 (Chivers Large Print)

The text of this Large Print edition is unabridged.
Other aspects of the book may vary from the original edition.

Set in 16 pt. Plantin by Minnie B. Raven.

Printed in the United States on permanent paper.

British Library Cataloguing-in-Publication Data available

Library of Congress Cataloging-in-Publication Data

Francis, Dorothy Brenner.
    Keys to love / Dorothy Brenner Francis.
        p.   cm.
    ISBN 0-7862-4036-9 (lg. print : hc : alk. paper)
    1. Key West (Fla.) — Fiction.   2. Boardinghouses —
Fiction.   3. Women artists — Fiction.   4. Grandmothers
— Fiction.   5. Large type books.   I. Title.
PS3556.R327 K49 2002
813'.54—dc21   2001050778

Keys to Love

Chapter One

I hid the letter in the pocket of my skirt where I could reach down and feel it whenever I needed to. I knew I was going to need to soon. Somehow touching the crisp paper gave me courage. And it was going to take courage to say what I had to say to Ron. Never before had any member of my family written to say that he needed me. Knowing that one is needed can be a heady sensation.

But Ron wasn't here yet. I had a few minutes' reprieve. My bangs felt heavy on my forehead, and I brushed them aside as I stood back to appraise my art work, to add a final touch to the colorful advertising layout I had been slaving over for so long. Orton's Onion Rings. I scowled. Would my picture persuade the Great American Public to rush to their nearest supermarket for Orton's Onion Rings?

As I packed my art supplies away, I glanced out my window. That spruce tree at the corner of the house was unique — its needles drooping under the weight of snow, a cardinal perched like a scarlet ornament on a topmost branch. Was there time to sketch it? I glanced at my watch. No. There wasn't time. There never was enough time. How I would like to have a whole day or maybe a whole lifetime to paint just what I wanted to paint. No more onion rings. No more ads for denture adhesives. Maybe the letter in my pocket would make those wishes come true.

"Anyone home?" Ron Baker burst into my apartment without knocking. "Dr. Baker at your service."

"Come in, Ron. You're early." I tried to ignore the fact that Ron was already in, that he was already lighting the silver-bowled pipe that he had confided to me he thought set off his fair coloring and blue eyes and enhanced his "young doctor" image.

"Finish the onion assignment?" Ron glanced at the layout.

I nodded. "At long last."

"Since you've reached the end of an assignment, it surely must be the perfect time for us to get married. How about it, Allison?" Ron put his arm around me and tilted my chin until I looked up at him. "Why not forget this silly art business and settle down to being Mrs. Ron Baker, wife of New York's most outstanding doctor?"

Reaching into my pocket, I touched the letter as I squirmed from Ron's embrace. "Don't rush me, Ron. I'm simply not ready to be married yet. Try to understand. I want to be somebody, to prove myself."

"Marry me before someone else sweeps me off my feet and you will be somebody. You'll be the wife of the handsomest doctor in town."

"Ron, I'm going to Key West day after tomorrow. I'm taking my two-week vacation." There! I had said it. I pulled the letter from my pocket and thrust it at Ron.

Allamanda House
114 Orchid Street
Key West, Florida

Dear Allison,

I am asking a favor of you. I need your help. If you could come to Key West for just a week or two, it would mean much to me.

I am being forced to sell Allamanda House. I am in no danger, yet I feel threatened. If your father were in the States, I would call on him. But that is impossible, so I am asking this favor of you.

There will be work to be done — the clearing away of a lifetime collection of odds and ends. But more than help with the work, I need the moral support of family.

Please advise me of your decision soon. I am looking forward to seeing you once again.

Love,
Gram

"I suppose you feel you must go," Ron said, irritation grating in his voice.

"Yes," I said. "It's such a strange letter. Why is Gram forced to sell? Why does she feel threatened?"

"Two weeks isn't forever, I suppose." Ron sighed.

Again I touched the letter, hoping for courage. "I'm going for at least a year, Ron, and maybe I'll stay in Florida permanently. I've asked for and been granted a transfer to the Acme Agency's Miami office. Gram needs me near her. She's always been the dependent sort, the kind of person who hates making decisions. I'm flattered that she's written to me."

"But you can't do that!" Ron exclaimed. "What about us? You're being immature, Allison."

"Perhaps it would be even more immature to stay in New York with a job that I
hate. I've been with Acme over two years.
In another year I'll have saved quite a bit
of money. If I live simply, I'll have enough
put by to see me through a whole year of
unemployment. At that time I'm going to
Key West, find an ivory tower, and paint to
my heart's content. In the meantime I'll be
only a hundred miles or so from my grandmother. If she needs me, I can go to her."

"You can't do this to me." Ron stood up.
"I thought we had an understanding."

"I'm sorry, Ron. Really I am. But I've
been telling you how I feel about you and
about art and about marriage for over a
year. You seem to listen, but you never really hear anything you don't care to hear."

I pulled a photo album from my book-
case. Flipping through the heavy black
pages, I stopped at a picture of my grandmother.

"Bunella Blue." Ron read the name
under the picture.

"My grandmother." I smiled. "Her nick-
name's Bunny. It's really quite fitting."

"You don't look a thing like her," Ron
said lamely.

"I take after Mom's side of the family.
The Baxters are all tall, brown-haired,

11

brown-eyed people." I turned another page in the album. "Here's a shot of Mom and Dad." To my surprise I felt tears in my eyes.

"What's the matter?" Ron asked. "Homesick?"

"I've really never had a home to be homesick for. Sometimes it seems as if that photo album is the only family I've ever known. When your parents are foreign missionaries, you don't see a lot of them. I can hardly remember the time when I lived with my family on a day-to-day basis."

"But you had your summers with your family," Ron reminded. "Even though you were sent to boarding schools, you had your summers."

"That's true. I feel like a heel when I get in a complaining mood like this. But I want you to understand why I have to go to Key West, to the only relative I have in the States. Gram is my family and she needs me. I haven't seen her for thirteen years. She visited me once in boarding school."

"But I need you, too," Ron said. "Every doctor needs a pretty, talented wife. You could do a lot for my practice, Allison."

"I'm sorry, Ron. My mind's made up. I'm leaving New York."

Suddenly Ron jumped up. His voice was coarse and loud. "Don't expect me to sit around waiting for you to come back from this wild chase to your grandmother's, Allison. There are plenty of good-looking girls in New York who would be happy to be a doctor's wife. I'll not sit around waiting for you to come to your senses."

Clamping his pipe between his teeth, Ron left the apartment, banging the door behind him.

I sighed. Why was it that every time a person made a major decision other people were hurt? I hadn't wanted to hurt Ron. I tried to explain the why of my decision, but he made no effort to understand. In a way I was relieved. A clean break was better than a half break that left tag ends dangling behind.

Again I touched my grandmother's letter and again I asked myself the same questions. Was Gram in danger? If there was no danger, why did she feel threatened? Would I be in danger if I went to Allamanda House? I mulled over the questions as I pulled my suitcases from the closet and began packing.

13

Chapter Two

I had thought that leaving New York would be difficult. But once I actually made the decision to go, my mind focused on its new goal and I was surprised at how easy departing could be. My superior at the Acme Agency had accepted my transfer with regret but without a fuss, and my landlady had another tenant waiting for my apartment almost before I had finished packing.

If I had learned one thing from my parents, it was to avoid collecting trivia. I was proud to be able to pack my lifetime possessions into my green Volkswagen. On Monday morning as I sat in the car for a moment before beginning my journey, I was tempted to call Ron.

But no. That would never do. This was the way I wanted to leave New York — free — with no ties binding me. If Ron and I were intended for each other, fate would bring us together again.

I traveled all day, slept overnight at a small motel, and then drove on at dawn. As the miles fell behind me, I emerged from snow and cold into a warmth that I found almost unbelievable for late December. Gradually I peeled off a cocoon of winter clothing, feeling light and free as a butterfly. After another motel stay I drove through Miami and into the Keys. Here the oceanside highway was a silver thread stitching island to island until at last I reached Key West.

I knew I would have to stop and ask for directions to Allamanda House, but I delayed as long as I could, drinking in the tropical beauty around me. On either side of the highway palm-shaded motels and hotels jeweled with purple bougainvillea and golden hibiscus blossoms studded the bay area. At an outdoor cafe overlooking the sea, gulls screamed and swooped down to snatch tidbits of bread thrown to them by vacationing children. I inhaled the sweet salt scent of the Gulf Stream as I parked my Volkswagen under a coconut palm, approached a service station attendant, and asked the way to Allamanda House.

After giving intricate directions, the station attendant scratched his head. "It's in Conch Town, but you won't get lost, ma'am. This island's too small for that."

"Thank you, sir." I began to repeat the

directions to be sure I understood them, but suddenly the attendant looked across the street and beckoned to a voluptuous girl wearing a midriff top, tight red shorts, and thongs.

"Hey, Vondetta! Going home?"

I watched as the red-haired girl headed in our direction, her swaying steps matching the rhythm of her jaws as she chewed a wad of gum. When Vondetta reached us, she gazed at the attendant from under sooty false lashes until he spoke to me.

"Miss, this is Vondetta Dewey. She lives at Allamanda House. If you're willing to give her a ride, she'll direct you to the right address."

I inhaled the cloying scent of heliotrope perfume that wafted around Vondetta. "Thank you." I nodded to the attendant. Then, smiling at Vondetta, I added, "I don't want to put you out. Are you sure you have time to ride to Allamanda House with me?"

"Sure thing, Miss — ah . . ."

"Miss Blue. Allison Blue. I've come to visit my grandmother."

"Bunny Blue's your grandmother?" Vondetta stopped chewing long enough to appraise me carefully.

"Yes, she is," I said. "I don't want to inconvenience you, Vondetta. If you aren't going to Allamanda House right now, I'm sure I can find it on my own."

"Oh, it's no trouble," Vondetta said. "My car's on the grease rack across the street. I was going to have to walk home or hitch a ride. This is a good deal for me. I'm on my feet all night at the Sea View House as it is. I'm glad to get a lift."

I thanked the station attendant, led the way back to the Volkswagen, and opened the door for Vondetta. Had Vondetta been a stock character in a high-school play I would have recognized her immediately as the flashy woman whose hard shell masked a heart of gold. But this was no play. Vondetta was for real and I couldn't be sure about her heart.

"So you live at Allamanda House," I said, sliding under the steering wheel. "I didn't know Gram had a companion."

"Companion?" Vondetta shrugged. "Never thought of myself in that role. Bunny Blue has taken in roomers as long as I've known her. There are four of us living there right now. Don't know where she's going to put you."

"I'm sure she has a place in mind or she wouldn't have invited me." I felt my hackles rise. Why did I feel that I had to defend myself to this girl? Traffic became heavier as Roosevelt Boulevard merged into Truman Avenue, but I divided my attention between it and Vondetta.

"I'm glad Gram has opened her home to young girls," I said. "It's probably a good arrangement for all of you."

"Who said anything about young girls?" Vondetta snorted and inspected a long, scarlet fingernail. "I'm eighteen and I'm the only girl at Allamanda House."

"Oh." I paused. "Who are the other roomers? I mean, what sort . . ."

Vondetta seemed to swell with importance as she began spouting information. "There's Ryan Bell. He runs a fishing boat. Nice guy if you like his type. And there's Jason McKillum, the history teacher. But just remember, I saw Jason first. And you'll get a hoot out of Gilda Fotopolus. She's a sponger."

"She sponges off Gram?" I asked, puzzled.

"Naw. She's a real sponger. Goes out spearing sponges from the ocean floor. That broken-down boat of hers looks worse than some of the wrecks the Cuban refugees escape on. Hey, we're almost there. Turn right at the next corner and it's the first house on your left."

I was half glad and half sorry that our ride was ending. I wanted to know Vondetta better, but at the same time I wanted to see Gram and renew family ties.

"Park here at the curbing," Vondetta said. "Allamanda House hides behind that tangle of tropical greenery across the street."

I looked to my left. Vondetta was correct. Allamanda House did seem to be hiding. All I could see of it above the dense growth of palms and pines was some broken balusters on what seemed to be a second-story porch, some third-floor windows, and a widow's walk perched atop the tin roof. Although the neighboring houses were close together on small lots, Allamanda House was different. A large garden surrounded it on all sides.

"Want me to help lug in some of your stuff?" Vondetta asked.

"No, thanks, Vondetta. I'll get it later. Right now I'm eager to see my grandmother again after all these years." In spite of my eagerness I felt a sense of foreboding as I strolled slowly across the street, then paused at a high cement wall set with a sculptured gatepost and a spiked, wrought-iron gate. From behind the cement wall a profusion of cacti stretched spiny prongs skyward as if guarding some secret retreat. Now I could see no house behind the cacti, so flamboyant was the tropical growth of ferns and palms and philodendrons.

"Does someone raise these?" I reached to touch a thorny cactus branch, and as I did so a bird squawked overhead and rustled the palm leaves in its flight from the garden. I jerked my hand back, startled.

Vondetta shrugged. "Bunny likes the cactus. She planted them there. If you think they're bad, you should see the night-blooming cereus. I call them vampire plants."

"Vampire plants," I muttered.

"Yeah." Vondetta opened the creaky gate. "I call them vampire plants because they bloom best at midnight under a full moon. Unnatural! But this isn't their blooming season. Come on, I'll show you the way to the house."

I followed Vondetta along a red, brick-paved path that twisted through the dense growth. In places we had to duck to avoid gnarled limbs and trailing vines. Although the sun was shining, this garden at Allamanda House was gloom-ridden and shaded. Eerie shadows snaked across our path wherever fingers of sunlight managed to filter through the rank growth. I inhaled a dank-earth smell. I didn't wonder that my grandmother felt threatened. This garden was enough to spook anyone.

"If you'll look to your left, you'll see some interesting, long fruit dangling from Bunny's sausage trees," Vondetta said.

I peered through a maze of trees and shrubs, seeing nothing unusual. Then, stepping from the path, I did spot the sausage tree. The foot-long fruits looked like something from another world. I touched one of them. Then, when I stepped back onto the path, I was alone. Vondetta had disappeared. I was confused. The path forked and I had no idea which way to go.

"Vondetta?"

No reply. How ridiculous! Why should I be afraid in my grandmother's garden? I chose a trail and followed it until I reached a cul-de-sac where the wild growth crawled rampantly over the concrete wall and tiny brown lizards scampered from my path.

I shuddered. Turning, I retraced my steps until I came to a waist-high circular wall. A well? I peeked into the enclosure. The hole was only five or six feet deep. But at the bottom gray-brown snakes slithered across the damp ground.

"Vondetta!" My voice shrilled in spite of my attempt to be calm.

"What is it?" Vondetta spoke quietly as she stepped from behind a philodendron-covered palm. "I just went to the potting shed to pick you an orchid."

My hand shook as I reached to take the lavender blossom. Although Vondetta was smiling, something in her eyes revealed that she had intended to abandon me, to frighten me.

"You won't get lost if you follow the white arrows Bunny has poked into the ground to mark the route to the house." Vondetta moved on ahead of me. "Follow me."

As I sidestepped from the path to avoid a dangling spider web, I tripped and almost fell.

"What's that?" I demanded, regaining my balance and pointing to the heavy wire I had stumbled over.

"That's just the cable," Vondetta replied. "There's the house right ahead of us. On either end of the house a cable stretches from roof to ground, lashing the house to the earth. It helps prevent damage when the winds come. Guess it works — the place hasn't blown away yet."

I shuddered as a cool, damp breeze wafted against my cheeks and I saw a clear view of Allamanda House for the first time. I don't know what I had been expecting, but certainly not this huge, decaying structure hidden in a loathsome garden.

The unpainted walls of Allamanda House towered three stories high. I had studied enough architectural design in college art classes to recognize that the widow's walk perched on top of the tin roof had been borrowed from New England. And surely the overhanging eaves and the gutters that connected with underground cisterns must have come from the drought-ridden West Indies. Allamanda House boasted Greek Revival columns that supported the second story porch, and the gables and window bays had to have been borrowed from the Gothic era.

"Well, don't just stand there." Vondetta nudged me with her elbow. "Go ahead and knock on the front door. Bunny's home. I live on the second floor. See you later."

Vondetta smiled, then dashed up the outside stairs to the second-story porch and disappeared through a doorway.

The wooden-shuttered windows across the front of Allamanda House reminded me of heavy-lidded, watching eyes. I tip-toed across the porch, paused a moment, then rapped lightly on a wooden door that looked as if it might once have been painted yellow.

I waited a long time. Then I knocked again. The door opened so quickly that I stepped back in surprise.

"Allison!" Gram rushed onto the porch, gave me a hug, then stood back to look up at me. "You look just like your picture, and you're a perfect image of your mother. I'd have known you anywhere. Come in! Come in and have a cool drink. I've been expecting you since early morning."

I followed Gram inside, liking her immediately. Although her face was seamed and windburned, her bright blue eyes glowed with friendly lights. We walked through a living room, a dining room, and into a kitchen where Gram pulled out a maple chair for me.

"I'll have a spot of Key limeade for you in a second," Gram said.

I relaxed. Gram looked almost as I had expected. Only a wiriness that I remembered was absent. Gram was plump and soft as a cream puff. She wore her fine, marshmallow-white hair in gentle waves around her face.

"Did you have any trouble finding me?" Gram asked, breaking into my thoughts.

"No trouble at all," I replied. "I've met Vondetta Dewey and she brought me here, I didn't know you rented out rooms."

"Guess I forgot to mention it." Gram shrugged. "But you'll meet all my tenants at noon. I've invited them all to a get-acquainted lunch — all except Ryan Bell. He's out on the *Blue Dolphin*." Gram set a frosted glass in front of me, plunked another glass down across the table, and then sat down.

"I'm so glad you've come, Allison. It means so much to me. It's hard to part with a house you've lived in a lifetime. Having family near will make it easier."

"Must you sell?" I asked, taking a sip of my drink.

"Yes." Gram nodded. "I've inured myself to face what must be done. But let's talk of other things for now. Tell me about New York, about your trip down here."

"There's nothing much to tell," I said. "I wrote you of my vacation and my transfer to Miami. I was delighted to come to Key West and the weather's marvelous. Simply wonderful! I'm surprised all New Yorkers haven't learned of this paradise and moved here en masse." I didn't tell Gram I was referring to the island, not to Allamanda House and its dreadful garden.

We lingered over our limeades for many minutes before I asked Gram to lead me back to my car. She seemed surprised at my request, but she came outside with me.

"Just follow the white arrows, Allison." Gram led the way, and we reached the garden gate in about a fourth of the time it had taken when Vondetta played guide. Again I felt sure that Vondetta had tried to frighten me.

When Gram walked with me through the garden, it seemed less eerie. After three trips across the street to the car and back I had most of my baggage assembled on the weather-worn porch of Allamanda House.

"I suppose you're thinking that Allamanda House needs a paint job," Gram said.

I blushed. Was Gram reading my mind? "It could use a face lift," I said. "But, really, I was wondering why you called the place Allamanda House."

"That was its name when I bought it," Gram replied. "The allamanda is one of the most popular vines in these out islands. It bears showy, trumpet-shaped blossoms in a lemon-yellow hue. If you look carefully, you can tell that the house was once trimmed in yellow — the shutters, the porch ceiling. I'd have it repainted, but it's quite an expensive job and the salt air seems to lick paint right from the boards."

"Where shall I put my things?" I asked, smiling. "Vondetta hinted that you might be hard put to find a place for me."

"Vondetta!" Gram snorted. "She knows good and well that there's an empty room right down the hallway from her. There's even a storage closet at the end of the hallway where you can keep your easel and other art equipment."

I started to carry a suitcase inside, but Gram stopped me. "Your room will be up-stairs, Allison. We'll use this outside stairway. It's the only one. When the old-time carpenters built these homes, their aim was to conserve inside space. That's why the stairway's out here."

Gram beckoned me to follow her up the sturdy steps, onto the second-floor porch with its broken balusters, and on through the doorway that led into a narrow hall with five rooms opening off it. As we walked down the hall, we came to a scant staircase, more like a ship's companionway than the stairs in a private home. I glanced upward.

"Third floor?"

Gram nodded. "Nothing up there but storerooms. That's what I want you to help me with once you get settled."

Gram led me to the last room that opened off the hallway. It was dim and shadowy until Gram opened the shutters. This second floor to Allamanda House rose above part of the garden vegetation, and bright sunlight streamed through the side windows. I was delighted until I noticed a dead gull lying on the windowsill, its stiff body covered with black insects.

I turned my back on the window before Gram noticed my dismay, and I tried to ignore the musty smell that hung in the room. Clearly this space had been unused for a long time. After I flopped my suitcase down on a brass bedstead, I glanced around the room. Walking to one wall, I ran my fingers over the wooden paneling.

"It's so different," I said. "I noticed that all the walls and ceilings downstairs are made of wood. Was Allamanda House built before people knew about plaster?"

"No, indeed," Gram said. "This house was built over a hundred years ago in the Bahamas. The wooden walls and ceilings are better able to stand hurricane gales than plaster ones. When Key West became the major shipwrecking depot in the Caribbean, the sea captain who built Allamanda House knocked it apart and shipped it from Exuma in the Bahamas to Key West. He rebuilt it here and carried on his salvage business from this island."

"Imagine taking a house apart and putting it together again as if it were a jigsaw puzzle!"

"People claim it wasn't too difficult a job," Gram said. "The house has no metal nails in it. It's fitted together with wooden pegs and points." Gram went to the closet and opened the door to reveal empty hangers and lots of space. "I'll leave you alone to unpack and rest for a few minutes. You make yourself right at home, Allison. Come lunchtime, I'll send for you."

I smiled, and as Gram left me I wondered if Allamanda House might not be my ivory tower, my special place to paint. But that was silly. Gram was preparing to sell the house. That was why I had come here to the island — to help her.

Chapter Three

For a few moments I tried to relax on the bed. Everything about Allamanda House was old-fashioned, and the paneled walls and ceiling made me feel as if I were trapped in a wooden box.

As I let my eyes wander over the heavy oak chest, dressing table, and desk, I wondered idly if Ron missed me. I couldn't truthfully say that I had missed him. My mind had been caught and held first by the eerie garden and now by this unusual room.

When at last I started unpacking, I found myself wishing that Gram hadn't arranged a get-acquainted lunch quite so soon. We had hardly had time to visit at all, and I knew nothing important could be discussed before outsiders. Was someone in this strange household forcing Gram to sell? I promised myself to ask her at the first opportunity.

I had barely started unpacking my cosmetic case when Vondetta called to me from the hallway, her voice throaty and low. "Bunny says come on down, Allison. Lunch is ready."

"Be with you in a sec." I smoothed my long hair with a brush, pulled it back from my face with a green headband, then tied a silk scarf printed with four-leaf clovers around my neck. The scarf had been a gift from my parents, and I had always considered it sort of a talisman. I wore it most of the time. Smoothing the scarf into place, I joined Vondetta on the upper porch.

Vondetta led me to the shuttered dining room where a handsome man and an elderly lady waited beside a round oak table spread with a lime-green cloth. In the dimness Gram was hurrying from kitchen to table, her seamed face flushed with excitement as well as from the heat.

"Please sit down, everyone." Gram adjusted a window shutter to admit the light. "Make yourselves at home. Just sit anywhere."

I noticed that Vondetta went out of her way to sit by the tall, brooding man on her right. Gram waited until everyone was seated, then she spoke again.

"I want you all to meet my granddaughter, Allison Blue. Allison, on your left is Gilda Fotopolus, my dear old friend. Next to Gilda is Jason McKillum, and of course you've already met Vondetta."

"How do you do." I adjusted my chair at the table, and as I smiled at Gram's three housemates, my artist's eye sent capsule descriptions to my brain to be filed for future reference.

Gilda Fotopolus was a buxom, strapping woman with piercing brown eyes, who looked as tough and determined as a hungry shark. Vondetta's handsome friend, Jason McKillum, peered at us with smoldering black eyes deeply set under beetling brows. His nose had an interesting hump at its bridge, and Jason kept tugging down the sleeves of his turtleneck sweater, although the day was warm.

I squirmed in the awkward silence that followed my introduction. Silently Gram served conch chowder, while Gilda impaled me with a piercing gaze that demanded my full attention.

"You ever been sponging?" Gilda's voice was loud but indistinct, like a faulty public-address system. I could hear her, but she was hard to understand.

"No, I never have," I replied. "Vondetta told me that you're a sponger. It sounds quite interesting."

"You bet it is." Gilda tossed her head to emphasize her words, and I saw that she had two upper teeth missing and many silver fillings. The golden hoops dangling from her pierced ears swayed with the motion of her head, and covering her gray hair Gilda wore a black kerchief that matched the black one-piece coverall that encased her rawboned figure. I tried not to stare at her.

"I'm one of the best spongers in the Keys," Gilda said. "I'll take you out for a day in my skiff if you'd like to go. Most spongers work in pairs — one to pole the boat and one to spot the sponges. But I work alone."

"I'd love to go out with you sometime," I replied with more enthusiasm than I really felt. I had come here to help Gram and to settle down to a few days of serious painting. I couldn't let myself become involved with people who were interested in other things. Two weeks would pass before I knew it. But it had been a long time since I had taken a vacation. I decided to allow myself the luxury of becoming acquainted with Key West and the pastimes it offered.

I glanced at Jason McKillum, but I could think of nothing to say to him. He seemed quiet and withdrawn, and I blushed as I felt an unexpected attraction to him. "I saw him first." The echo of Vondetta's warning rang in my ears. Was Jason the reason Vondetta had tried to frighten me in the garden? Did she think she could scare me away from her man?

While I was struggling to think of some bit of conversation to interest Jason, Gram spoke again, her hands fluttering nervously to pat the wispy strands of hair that framed her face.

"Now that everybody's here — all except Ryan, that is — I have an announcement to make." Gram cleared her throat and every eye in the room bored into her. "You're all probably wondering why Allison is here. And you have every right to know because her presence will affect each of you. Allison has taken vacation time to come to Key West in order to help me clear out the third-floor storerooms. You see, I'm planning to sell Allamanda House. By the end of the week Jason may be the new owner unless, of course, someone else makes me a better offer for the place than he has."

The silence seemed to reverberate against the wooden walls. Then Gilda's eyes flashed sparks and she began firing questions.

"But what about the rest of us, Bunny? You can't just up and sell out. Where will we live?" Turning to Jason, Gilda demanded, "Will you go on renting rooms to us, Jason? Will you?"

Jason spoke for the first time during the meal, and I liked his low voice that rang like a bass chime.

"If I'm lucky enough to buy the house, I'm afraid you'll all have to find other places to live," Jason said. "I plan to restore Allamanda House to what it was during its heyday. I want to open it to the public as an historic museum."

After another brief silence Gilda and Jason continued talking and arguing, and I felt hostility in the air.

"I knew Bunny was going to sell all along," Vondetta whispered to me, clearly proud to have shared top-secret information. "Jason told me so at least a month ago. He knew I could keep my mouth shut."

I squirmed. I hadn't dreamed that Gram had been renting rooms or that selling Allamanda House would be of import to anyone outside the family. I was glad when the meal ended and the tenants returned to their own quarters.

"Oh, Allison!" Gram slumped in her chair once we were alone, fanning herself with her napkin. "How I hated telling them! I could never have done it without your moral support. But now they know, and it's a load off my mind."

"What about the man who isn't here?" I asked. "Ryan? Was that his name?"

"No, Ryan doesn't know yet, but Jason promised to tell him when he comes in from fishing tonight." Gram rose and began clearing away the luncheon things, and I hurried to help her, not knowing quite what to say. I had lots of questions to ask, but Gram seemed so distraught over her recent announcement that I decided to change the subject.

"The lunch was good, Gram. That conch chowder had a strange but pleasant taste. I'm sure everyone enjoyed it." We bustled between dining room and kitchen for a few moments, and washed and dried the dishes. Then Gram led the way to the front porch.

"Allison, I want you to see my garden. It's really the only thing about Allamanda House that I can hardly bear to leave."

As I followed Gram from the porch, I blurted the question that had been uppermost in my mind for so long. "Gram, who is forcing you to sell Allamanda House? Is this Jason McKillum threatening you in some way? I can tell that you're deeply attached to your house and garden. Why must you give the place up?"

"Jason is my good friend," Gram said, snapping a dead leaf from a croton plant. "Circumstances are forcing me to sell. That's all — circumstances. I simply can't meet my financial obligations any longer. Allamanda House is too much of a burden for me. Repair bills. Utility bills. Taxes. It's just more than I can manage."

"I wish I could help you keep the place." I bent to inhale the fragrance of an orchid blossom, but it was scentless.

"Nonsense, you have your own life to lead. I'm more than happy that you've taken a few days off to be with me, to help me out with the sorting and discarding chores. And I'm delighted that you'll be close by in Miami from now on."

As we walked through the junglelike garden, Gram spoke of other things, pointing out royal palms, hibiscus bushes, and poinsettia plants ablaze with scarlet.

"Come over here, but watch your step, Allison." Gram held my elbow and pointed to a low curbing where a crown-of-thorns plant grew. "This is an old cistern. There are several in the garden. There used to be other houses in this area before a hurricane blew them down. These cisterns are all that remain now."

Remembering the snakes in the other cistern, I shivered in spite of the warmth of the day. "Why don't you cap the cistern, Gram? Surely it's dangerous to leave them open like this."

"Oh, there's no danger," Gram said. "I lock the garden gate at night so strangers can't intrude. Everyone living here knows the cisterns' locations, and they're quite off the brick pathway. Besides, Jason keeps his turtles down there."

"Turtles?" I leaned over the wide mouth of the cistern, peering some fifteen feet or so into its dark depths. At the bottom of the hole I saw two turtles perched on a smooth rock. I tried to hide my revulsion behind a smile.

"Jason rescued the turtles from some kids on the beach," Gram explained. "The children had carved their initials on the turtles' shells, and Jason felt sorry for them because they had been disfigured. He feeds them well, and often he hauls them up in a bucket and lets them have the run of the garden for a day or so. Jason's a soft-hearted one — always sticking up for kids and animals."

I shuddered and stepped back onto the path. Behind the cistern a tree with orchidlike blossoms was in full bloom, and I tried to keep my attention focused on its beauty instead of on the deep, dank pit. Clearly Gram thought her garden a place of loveliness. I tried to see its beauty through her eyes, but I failed. This garden frightened me, chilled me with its dank odors and dark shadows.

Gram sighed. "The garden's really far from its best right now. But in February when the poincianas begin to bloom, it will blaze with color. Northerners think the tropics have no seasonal changes. They think of the islands in terms of year-around summer. But after a person has lived here for a while he learns to know when the different plants and trees and shrubs blossom. I couldn't bear to miss winter, summer, spring, or fall. Each season has a distinct beauty all its own. But enough of the garden. Let's go up-stairs. I'll show you the storerooms."

Willingly I followed Gram from the shadowed garden. We climbed the outer staircase to the second-floor porch, en-tered the hallway, and then climbed the ladderlike steps to the third floor. The landing at the top of the nearly vertical flight of steps was almost too narrow to stand on.

Gram wedged her plump form sideways around the banister to enter the room to our right. I did likewise, hanging on to the banister rail for safety.

"There's this room, and there's another room just like it on the other side of the stairs."

I felt perspiration on my upper lip as heat enveloped me like an eiderdown quilt. Standing on a chair, Gram opened a ceiling vent.

"That will let the hot air out," she explained. "Allamanda House has three of these roof hatches. Her carpenters borrowed the idea from their sailing ships. Another vent opens onto the widow's walk. It's in the closet and I seldom use it."

I glanced around the room at an array of items — boxes of books, statues, vases, old furniture, ancient magazines. Everything lay under a thick gray film of dust. And as I sneezed, it seemed to me that the clutter of a lifetime had been preserved in this stuffy-smelling room.

"Of course, a lot of these things can be thrown away," Gram said, blowing the dust from a tattered lampshade. "But it's the sorting that's important to me. Some things are of historical interest, and they must go to the library or to the Martello

Museum. I'm in charge of laundering the costumes on the wax figures in the period rooms of the museum, and once a month I take a committee of workers there after hours to help tidy up. Jason's the regular caretaker, but he does the heavy work — the yard, the floors. He usually spends his Sunday evenings there. My committee is due to work before long. You can help us, Allison. We can always use two more hands."

"Of course," I replied. "I'll be glad to help."

"You're surely not going to begin on this job today," a masculine voice said.

"Jason!" Gram exclaimed. "I didn't hear you come up the steps. No. We're not going to tackle either storeroom today. I was just showing Allison what lay ahead of us."

"In that case maybe you'll let me borrow your granddaughter for an hour or so." Jason smiled down at me. "Would you like to take a brief tour of Duval Street, Allison? It offers some interesting sights."

"I'd be delighted," I said, hoping that Jason couldn't hear my heart pounding. What ailed me, anyway? I wasn't the type to let a stranger sweep me off my feet so easily. I tried to forget Vondetta's warning that she had seen Jason first. Clearly Jason felt free to request my company.

"Let's go downstairs then," Gram said. "Watch your footing on those steps."

Once we reached the second floor, I excused myself long enough to freshen my makeup and slip into a cooler dress. Jason was waiting for me on the lower porch, and he led the way to his car and opened the door for me.

"Excuse me a moment, Allison. I forgot my sunglasses."

Jason was gone only a few seconds. When he returned, I asked, "You're on vacation from school?"

Jason nodded. "I teach history at the high school. Classes are still dismissed for the Christmas holidays, but we all go back in a day or two."

"How nice to have a winter vacation in such a charming place," I said. From the corner of my eye I saw Vondetta standing in the upper doorway watching our departure. Was Vondetta really Jason's girl friend, or was she merely hoping for that position?

"It really hasn't been much of a vacation," Jason said, easing into traffic and turning his head away from me in a peculiar sort of manner. "I moonlight by working as a custodian for the museum and I also work a few hours each week for the Ramsey Shrimp Company. The fleet goes out at this time of year, and they always need extra hands to maintain equipment or repair a boat or two in dry dock."

"Sounds like interesting work," I said.

"It's smelly, disagreeable work and I hate it." Jason pounded on the steering wheel to emphasize his words. "But the money's going to Bunny. Owning Allamanda House will make it all worthwhile."

"Allamanda House means so much to you?" I asked.

Jason parked the car near a busy street, helped me out, then guided me around the corner to a sidewalk cafe.

"I can't begin to tell you how much Allamanda House means to me," Jason said. "I've scrimped and saved for years in order to be able to buy it. It's an historical landmark, Allison. It deserves to be preserved and displayed. For all her good intentions Bunny dishonors the place by turning it into a common rooming house."

"What if someone makes a higher bid on it than you did?" I asked. "That could happen, you know."

"I try not to think of such a thing."

I sat down on the chair Jason pulled out for me. As he sat down directly across from

43

me, I noticed for the first time a scar running from his ear to the tip of his chin. The scar wasn't too noticeable, but Jason unknowingly attracted attention to it by trying to hide it with his hand.

"Key lime pie and Cuban coffee are the specialties of the house," Jason said before a waitress had time to bring a menu. "Want to try them?"

"Sounds great," I said.

As soon as Jason had given the waitress our order he began telling me about Key West, and I listened half hypnotized by his deep voice.

"When Spanish conquistadors began to search the Carribbean for gold, they discovered this small island," Jason said. "They called it Cayo Heuso, Bone Key, because it was covered with bones."

"What sort of bones?" I asked.

"Human bones." Jason shrugged. "Historians speculate that Indians once lived here and that an enemy tribe killed them off, left their bodies to rot, and departed."

"How horrible." Again I caught myself shivering.

Jason talked on, relating the histories of the island economy, the reef wrecking crews, the empire of cigar factories, and the devastating hurricanes. But all the time he talked he kept his head turned at a strange angle as if trying to hide his humped nose, and at the same time he kept one hand shielding the scar on his chin.

The waitress brought our pie and coffee, and I loved their unusual tastes. But the outstanding thing about this outing was Jason himself. Jason was an enigma and I wanted to know him better. He attracted me. I had never felt this way about Ron.

I had been so intrigued with Jason's tales of Key West history that I had hardly noticed our present setting — the sparkling bay in the distance, the whispering palms, the pelicans wheeling toward the sea. I tried to drink them all in, to memorize the scene in the few moments it took to walk back to the car.

By the time we reached Allamanda House, New York and Ron Baker seemed like names from some far-distant, half-remembered past. I thanked Jason for the pleasant time and reluctantly returned to my room.

I was still half mesmerized in a daydream of Jason McKillum and Key West when I saw the ugly writing soaped onto my dressing-table mirror.

"GET OUT, ALLISON BLUE! DANGER! GO HOME!"

Chapter Four

Horrified, I stared at the crudely smudged words. As I looked into the mirror, they seemed to be written on my forehead. Someone was warning me to get out — threatening me. Someone didn't want me here at Allamanda House. But who? Vondetta? Was Vondetta jealous because Jason had taken me out for coffee?

Storming downstairs, I raced across the lower porch and into the house. Rushing to Gram, I told her what had happened, somehow managing to keep my voice low in spite of my agitation.

"Come upstairs and see for yourself," I said. Then suddenly I felt frightened. "Gram! In your letter you said that you felt threatened. Has someone given you a similar warning?"

"Of course not," Gram replied. "You're jumping to conclusions. When I wrote that I felt threatened, I simply meant that I felt uneasy, unequal to facing the new and strange situation."

"Well, I've been threatened, Gram.

There's no doubt about it. I'd like to know who my enemy is. Maybe you'll recognize the writing."

Still frightened and worried, I dashed back up the outside stairway, then waited on the upper porch until Gram heaved her plump figure onto the landing. I hurried down the hallway and into my room, gesturing toward the mirror.

"What do you make of that, Gram?"

Gram studied the writing for a few moments before speaking. "I'm not sure just what to make of it, Allison. Of course I'm sorry that this has happened, but don't let it upset you. Someone living here is just angry because I'm selling Allamanda House, and he's taking his anger out on you because you've come to help me. Whoever did it will surely calm down once he gets used to the idea of someone else owning the house."

"But who could have done it?" I asked. "Which one of them do you think might have come sneaking in here while I was away?"

"It could have been any one of them, I suppose." Gram lowered her voice. "Gilda didn't go sponging today because of the noon luncheon, and Vondetta doesn't go to work until early evening. Those two have been home all afternoon as far as I know."

"I suppose it could have been Jason," I admitted reluctantly. "He left me in the car while he returned to the house for sunglasses. He would have had time. And what about that other fellow — Ryan? Is he home yet?"

Gram nodded. "Ryan came in a few minutes before you did. The fishing boats dock at Garrison Bight about four o'clock. I told him about selling the house. But don't worry, Allison. I'm sure this silly writing means nothing. Nothing at all. None of my roomers is dangerous. I've known them all for a long time. They're my friends, Allison. My good friends."

I wished I could believe Gram, but I was scared. "Is there a key to this door, Gram? I'd like to keep my door locked from now on."

"I'll see what I can find." Gram rubbed the writing from the mirror with the tail of her apron. "But I think a skeleton key will fit any of these old locks. Let's forget this for now and go out for a bite of supper. You'll feel better with a warm meal in your stomach."

"I'll cook if you want to eat here," I said, remembering Gram's words about financial difficulties.

"Tonight we eat out," Gram insisted.

"You needn't fancy up. Everyone dresses casually here on the island. I thought we'd go to the Sea View House where Vondetta works as a waitress. They serve excellent shrimp dinners."

I realized that Gram was only trying to take my mind off the warning on the mirror. Gram waited while I washed up and ran a comb through my hair. Then we took my Volkswagen and drove along the bayside road to the Sea View House.

Although I had no valuable possessions, I worried about leaving my room unlocked. What would happen in my absence? But once we were inside the restaurant, I tried to be cheerful. The pleasant aroma of coffee and the nautical wall decorations helped me forget my troubles. We waited near the doorway until a hostess dressed in a flowing red caftan seated us. Soon Vondetta came with pad in hand to take our order. In her skimpy, flared uniform and white patent boots Vondetta looked even younger than her eighteen years, but she was well aware of the many male glances that followed her.

I looked up as a tall man with curly dark hair and sea-gray eyes stopped at our table.

"Hey, Ryan!" a cook called from the kitchen.

"Hello, Ryan," a waitress purred. "How are you tonight?"

Ryan spoke to the cook and the waitress and nodded to people seated around us, clearly acquainted with almost everyone.

"May I join you, ladies?" Ryan asked, twirling a blue yachting cap on his left thumb. His voice was quiet but forceful, and I liked him instantly.

"Ryan!" Gram beamed with pleasure. "Of course you may join us. I've been wanting you to meet Allison, my granddaughter."

"Good evening, Allison." Ryan smiled.

I smiled back, entranced by Ryan Bell. I felt myself blushing because I suddenly had an embarrassing desire to impress Ryan, to let him know I was someone special. But how? I felt like an eight-year-old wanting to shout out, "Look at me! I can paint a picture."

"Allison's come to help me clear out the house," Gram said, unaware of my thoughts. "She has two weeks' vacation, but three days of it have flown by already."

"Will you sell to Jason?" Ryan asked, seemingly uninterested in my free time.

"I'm open for offers," Gram said. "I've made no promises. But Jason's made the best offer so far."

"I don't blame you, Bunny," Ryan said.

"You have to take the highest bid. That's just good business."

"You've had other offers?" I asked, feeling left out of the conversation.

"Ryan wanted the house," Gram replied. "But it just didn't work out for us to do business."

I smiled at Ryan, and suddenly I realized that everyone smiled at Ryan. He was that kind of a person. For some crazy reason I imagined him as a child with frogs in his pockets and stars in his eyes. But he was no child now, and he was scrutinizing me, his eyes dark and probing.

"Mind if I sketch you?" Ryan asked, pulling a pencil from his pocket and turning his paper place mat over to the blank side. "You have remarkable features."

Now I felt myself color with pleasure. "Gram didn't tell me you were an artist. I thought you were a fisherman." I smiled to myself, sensing that I wasn't the only one who felt insecure. Ryan Bell wanted me to know that he was someone special. He wanted me to know that he was an artist.

"I have a split personality," Ryan said with a grin, his gray eyes appraising me.

"That must have been your easel in the storage closet," I said. "Guess we'll have to share space."

"Allison's an artist, too," Gram said, speaking the words I was too modest to utter. "She works for an advertising agency in New York."

"In Miami now," I corrected. "Don't forget that I asked for a transfer and that it was granted. We'll get to see each other more often from now on. I'm going to love having some family nearby."

"Allison!" Gram exclaimed. "I hope I didn't cause you to change any of your career plans."

"Nothing of the sort, Gram. I wanted to leave New York. In fact I'd really like to leave commercial art. I know that the longer I stick with it, the harder it will be to break away. I think leaving New York was a step in the right direction. I may have more time in Miami for serious painting."

All the time we were talking, Ryan was sketching, and he finished the likeness of me just as Vondetta came to our table and plunked a cardboard box in front of him.

"One shrimp dinner to go," Vondetta said, making out Ryan's bill. Vondetta had no smile for Ryan, although I had seen her lavishing smiles and winks on all the other male customers. "Your order will be coming up soon, Bunny," Vondetta said. "Ryan telephoned in ahead. That's why his is ready first."

"We're in no hurry," Gram replied. "It's good to just sit and relax."

After Vondetta left us, Ryan finished his sketch and handed it to me.

"Ryan! That's good. It really is. It looks just like me."

"Keep it if you like," Ryan said, grinning. "Compliments of Captain Ryan Bell. What sort of things do you like to paint?" Ryan looked deep into my eyes, and I felt flustered and self-conscious.

"I like to do landscapes, seascapes, still life," I replied. "I like to paint any scene that is different — the chimney sweep who is about to fall, the pelican that is about to grab a fish."

"All I ask for is beauty," Ryan said, "and you make an excellent model. Your hair, your eyes, your facial bone structure — perfect. And that scarf with the lucky clovers adds a whimsical touch."

Before I could think of a glib reply, Ryan rose, picked up his hat and his box supper, and left us as quickly as he had arrived. I stared after him, disappointed at his departure, until Gram touched me on the elbow.

"Don't get excited over Ryan Bell, Allison. He reels out a long line and he's everybody's buddy — has to be to keep in business. But Ryan has few intimate friends, and right now he's completely soured on girls. If you're hunting a man, look to Jason. He's shown more interest in you today than he's shown in any girl since I've known him. Jason's a good fellow, and he knows how to handle his money."

"No matchmaking, please, Gram." I kept my voice light as I slipped the sketch Ryan had drawn into my shoulder bag, easing it in carefully so as not to wrinkle it or bend the corners. "And speaking of handling money, why don't you level with me about your financial difficulties? What's your biggest problem, Gram? It seems to me that Allamanda House should be a paying enterprise."

"It might be if I operated it properly," Gram said. "But I'm no business woman. I can't get the roomers to pay their rent."

Vondetta appeared with our meals, and I said no more until she served us and left. The shrimp was thinly battered, tender, and delicious, and I hated to pursue an unpleasant subject. But I felt that I must.

"Why can't you get your roomers to pay their rent, Gram? You said they were your friends. They all seem to be employed. Surely they pay something."

"Sometimes Vondetta pays a little, but she's way behind. I knew Vondetta's grandmother, Allison. I can't turn the girl out. Her parents are divorced; she's had a rough life. Now, Jason — he pays. I can depend on him. The first of every month Jason is there with his rent check. But Gilda is months behind, maybe even farther than Vondetta."

"What about Ryan Bell? Does Ryan pay?"

"Ryan and I have a deal," Gram replied. "He lets me ride the *Blue Dolphin* free in return for his room at Allamanda House."

"Big deal!" Anger blocked my throat until I couldn't swallow my food. "Why would you want to ride the *Blue Dolphin*?"

"To catch fish," Gram replied. "That's the only thing that's kept Allamanda House going this long — my fishing. I go out almost every day and I sell my catch to Ernie's Fish Market. I let on that fishing's just a hobby, but it's hard work. I can't keep it up any longer."

"Gram, I simply don't understand all this." Puzzlement replaced my anger. "Why are you allowing these people who claim to be friends to freeload on you like this? Why? You must have a reason."

"I've told you they're my friends. Let me

explain. My family was very poor when I was a child, but my poverty ended when I married your grandfather. He was in charge of part of the maintenance of Henry Flagler's overseas railroad that ran from the mainland to Key West. He earned good money and he gave me everything I could possible want. Then he was killed in the hurricane of thirty-five."

"I'm sorry," I said. "Let's not talk about it."

"It's all right," Gram said. "We must talk about it so you'll understand. I had no special education and no special money-making skills. But after your grandfather's death, I collected enough insurance money to buy Allamanda House and to have a nest egg left over. I felt that your grandfather had given his very life to make me happy, and I vowed that in his memory I would try to share, would try to continue his giving. I share my home to make my friends happy. Up until a few years ago it worked out well. Then prices seemed to skyrocket. The first thing I knew my nest egg was gone. I am only sorry that my sharing has to stop. I've thought it over carefully and selling is the easiest way out. If I no longer own Allamanda House, then Gilda, Ryan, and Vondetta won't expect me to provide a home for them."

"There must be some way to avoid this sale," I said.

"There is no way," Gram replied. "And, really, I'm not hunting a way. I'm getting too old to keep up such a big place. I'm rather looking forward to moving into a small efficiency apartment where I can settle down and relax, sleep in if I want to, let the dusting wait if I don't feel like working. But what about you? If you've given up your job in New York and trans-ferred to Miami, what are your future plans?"

I took a sip of water. Perhaps it was best for Gram to sell Allamanda House, yet I felt that all her explanations failed to cover her reluctance to give the place up. I thought of the sale with mixed emotions.

"I'm quite unsure of my plans, Gram. I'd like to save enough money to take about a year off from commercial art. I'd like to paint, to exhibit if I could arrange it, and to see if there's any chance that I could make it on my own as a painter instead of a commercial artist. But I'll have to work a while in Miami before that dream will come true."

"When it does come true maybe we can share a small apartment here on the island." Gram sipped her coffee, then added more sugar. "Would you like that?"

"I'd love it," I said. "Some day I plan to hole up and paint and let the rest of the world go by. Will we start clearing out those storerooms tomorrow?"

"No, not tomorrow, Allison. I thought we'd go out on Ryan's *Blue Dolphin* tomorrow. I need the money from a good catch, and I want you to have a bit of vacation before we begin working on Allamanda House. Even if you care nothing for fishing, a day's outing on the boat will do you good. It will be a beautiful trip and a pleasant day."

"Whatever you say," I agreed. "However, two weeks' vacation time will run out before we know it. I want to help as much as I can while I'm here." I laughed. "I talk about working, but right now I'm so comfortably full of shrimp and so sleepy that all I want to do is go to bed."

"Then let's go home," Gram said. "You've had a big day, and we'll have to get up early in the morning."

I insisted on paying our bill. Then, outside in the warm evening air, I inhaled the scent of the Gulf Stream and imagined that I could taste salt spray on the breeze. But once we were back in the car, Allamanda House loomed in my mind like a bad dream. What might be awaiting me this time? Tomorrow I would buy a bolt for the inside of the door. That would be better than the skeleton key Gram had given me. A bolt would at least give me full security while I was inside the room.

Chapter Five

After preparing for bed I locked my door with the skeleton key Gram had provided. Then, for good measure, I dragged a desk in front of the doorway.

"If anyone tries to get in at least I'll hear him," I muttered to myself.

Lying in bed, I stared into the darkness and thought about all the people I had met that day. Which one of them had crept into my room to soap that horrid message onto my mirror?

Surely I could eliminate Jason from my list of suspects. Everything was going Jason's way. In all likelihood, Gram would be selling Allamanda House to him. He should be happy to have me here to help speed the moving process.

It surprised me to realize how relieved I was to have Jason in the clear. He attracted me more than any man I had ever met. What was it about him? Jason was handsome, but I had known lots of handsome men. Perhaps his brooding air of solitude, his aura of mystery were the characteristics that made him unique. Yet something about Jason didn't add up. He lived in one of Gram's inexpensive rooms, yet he had enough money to buy Allamanda House. Jason was a puzzle.

Would Ryan have tried to frighten me? I doubted that he would. Ryan seemed too open and aboveboard to go sneaking around writing warnings on mirrors. Yet I had learned that no one is an open book, not even Ron back in New York. Everyone is a bit unpredictable. Ryan Bell could bear watching.

Gilda? If one went by looks, Gilda might seem to be the guilty one. She was big. She was tough. And she was probably used to getting her own way. But looks could be deceiving. The culprit could just as easily be Vondetta. Gilda and Vondetta both stood to lose their soft living accommodations.

I wished I knew more about Vondetta. Clearly she was making a grandstand play for Jason. Vondetta had scowled as she watched Jason and me leave Allamanda House this afternoon. Maybe Vondetta had two reasons for wanting me out of the way.

I tried to ease the tangle of questions from my mind as I closed my eyes to sleep. But just as I was dozing, something awakened me. I jerked to a sitting position, listening. Had someone tried my door? I held my breath. No. I heard the sound again. Someone was walking about in the third-floor room directly above me. Perhaps Gram couldn't wait to start sorting her mementos. I relaxed.

The next thing I knew my alarm clock was jangling. I dressed hurriedly in cotton slacks and a long-sleeved shirt. Then I shoved the desk from in front of my door, relieved that no one had tried to enter. Stuffing suntan lotion, makeup, and my scarf into my shoulder bag, I locked my door and went downstairs.

"Good morning, Allison," Gram called from the kitchen. "Come have some breakfast. I'm packing a bite for our lunch."

Sunshine warmed the car as we drove to the docks with Gram directing the way.

"The *Blue Dolphin* ties up at Garrison Bight," Gram said. "It's almost landlocked, and it's the safest place for a boat when the winds blow."

I parked the car in a nearby lot and we walked the short distance to the docks. Tourists already crowded the sidewalk near the fishing boats. I gasped in pleasure when Gram stopped in front of a gleaming white boat trimmed with touches of blue.

Painted letters on the stern declared its name: the *Blue Dolphin*. Overhead a sign listed fares and designated Ryan Bell as the boat's captain.

I followed Gram to the end of a short dock, up a narrow gangplank, and onto the *Blue Dolphin*. Gram claimed a place near the bow of the boat by fitting her fishing rod into an empty socket and plunking her lunch sack on the bench behind it.

"This is fabulous!" I exclaimed. "Ryan Bell must be wealthy."

Gram laughed. "Hardly. He only has a small equity in the boat and the payments are astronomical. That's why he couldn't match Jason's offer to buy Allamanda House."

"It's still fabulous," I insisted.

"Yes, it is," Gram agreed. "Ryan's father was captain of a turtle boat back in the days when turtling was big business. Ryan has always tried to live up to his father's image. Times have changed, but Ryan's going to make it on his own. I'm sure of it."

"Look at those pelicans!" I pointed to the wise-looking birds, who returned my gaze with unblinking eyes. "And smell that salt air. I never realized that the sea was so green."

"It'll be dark blue when we get out in deep water," Gram said. "But now that I've secured my place here, we're free to go to the upper deck. View's better from up there."

"Lead the way," I said.

We climbed narrow steps to the top deck, and while Gram relaxed on a reclining chair, I stood gazing at the scene at hand, wishing I could memorize every detail. Fishing boats similar to the *Blue Dolphin* were docked on either side of us, and the ticket sellers shouted at the crowds.

"Ride the *Blue Dolphin* for a big catch!"

"The *Can't Miss* brings 'em in!"

The *Blue Dolphin* was the first boat to fill its quota of forty-seven passengers, and soon the engines roared. I saw a white cloud of vapor waft from the stern at the same time I smelled the odor of diesel fuel. The engines vibrated the floorboards of the deck, making my feet tingle.

In a moment Captain Ryan Bell appeared on the upper deck, smiled and waved to his passengers, then entered the wheelhouse. Before I realized it we had pulled away from the dock and were heading across the bight toward the Gulf of Mexico.

"Shouldn't you go down to your fishing

place?" I asked Gram.

She shook her head. "We'll stop to take on fuel, then we'll travel an hour or so before Ryan reaches the spot where we'll fish. I may as well relax up here. I get tired sitting on that backless bench all day long."

"Gram! You should have been resting last night instead of fooling around up in the storeroom."

"What do you mean?" Gram asked. "I went to bed just as soon as you went upstairs. I had a good sleep."

"But I heard you." I stopped speaking as the full meaning of Gram's words hit me. "I heard someone walking around in the room directly over my bed, Gram. I'm sure of it. The boards creaked and squeaked, and I heard footsteps."

"You must have imagined it, Allison. Nobody goes up there except me. Nobody has any reason to go up. There's nothing there but junk and personal mementos."

I said no more, but I knew I had heard someone in the storeroom. Either someone had been sneaking around on the third floor last night or Allamanda House was inhabited by ghosts. And I didn't believe in ghosts.

We rode a while in silence. Then Gram rose. "I'd better go down now. If you have any questions, just go on in the wheel-house and ask Ryan. There's a cushioned bench in there, and you might find some of his navigating instruments interesting."

I watched Gram ease herself from the stairway that rolled and pitched with the movement of the boat. Ryan attracted people like nectar attracts bees, and a crowd already filled the wheelhouse. But I decided that Ryan wouldn't mind one more, so I walked inside and sat down on the bench behind his chair.

"Good morning, Allison! Didn't know you were here." Ryan's gray eyes glowed like moonstones as he spoke, giving me the impression that he was genuinely glad to see me.

"Gram talked me into coming along, and I'm glad she did. You have a marvelous boat. It must be quite exciting to roam the ocean every day."

"We're in the Gulf," Ryan corrected. "And it gets to be routine. It's just like any job a person does day in and day out. But I like it. There's always an element of surprise."

"Do you like fishing better than sketching or painting?" I asked. "I think you have real talent."

Ryan shrugged. "My family has always

been seafaring. Operating the *Blue Dolphin* makes the sketching and painting possible."

"Have you ever tried making a living just by painting?"

"Nope. Never have. Guess I like being with people too much to hide away in some Front Street studio and do nothing but paint."

"I don't know about a Front Street studio," I said, "but I'd like to do just that — hide away somewhere and paint. Maybe I'll find an ivory tower."

Ryan shrugged. "An ivory tower could be awfully lonely."

I forced a smile, wondering why Ryan was going out of his way to antagonize me. He hadn't seen any of my work. Who was he to discourage me from trying to make a living by painting? Neither of us spoke for a long time, but my thoughts raced. Perhaps Ryan was trying to discourage me so I would leave Key West sooner. He had wanted to buy Allamanda House, and here I was hastening it into someone else's hands.

In a surge of brashness that I didn't know I possessed, I rose and walked across the wheelhouse to a position where I could see Ryan's face.

"Someone was prowling in my room at Allamanda House yesterday, Ryan. Do you know anything about it?"

Ryan met my gaze, his gray eyes now flinty and grim. "Why should I know anything about it? What was stolen?"

"Nothing was stolen. There was a warning soaped onto my dressing-table mirror. A warning that I was in danger if I remained at Allamanda House, or perhaps even in the Keys."

Ryan shrugged.

In that moment I saw Ryan through the red haze of my anger. Here I had revealed my uneasiness, my fear, and Ryan's only reaction was a shrug. Why did he resent me? Why was he erecting this invisible wall between us? I quickly left the wheelhouse and sat down on a deck chair until I calmed down.

"Shark!"

The cry rang over the boat. "Shark! Shark!" I jumped up, and as I ran to peer over the side of the deck to watch the man who had hooked the monster, I almost collided with Ryan. He brushed me aside, rushed into a cabin, then darted onto the deck with a rifle.

"Ryan!" I shouted as fear replaced curiosity. "What's the matter?"

Ryan ignored me. Through narrowed lids he watched the taut line in the water as the man played the shark from one side of the boat to the other. The rest of the fishermen reeled their tackle in to avoid tangles.

With the rifle barrel pointed skyward, Ryan hurried to the lower deck. As the man reeled the shark to the surface, Ryan aimed and fired. I flinched at three sharp reports. The shark thrashed for a moment, then lay motionless on the surface of the sea, blood oozing from its wounds.

The shooting was over in a moment. The crew began heaving the shark on board, and the passengers crowded close to see the catch. But I wasn't interested in the shark. The wind blew cold, and I buttoned my sweater and tied my scarf on my head as I studied Ryan Bell. My attention was riveted to this man who could use a rifle with such ruthless precision.

Chapter Six

I huddled on the bench beside Gram during the rest of the fishing trip, thinking of the hair-thin line that separates life from death. When we docked at Garrison Bight that afternoon, I welcomed the comforting feeling of land beneath my feet.

Ernie's Market had sent a man in a truck to buy fish from anyone who wanted to sell. Tourists crowded around, and I watched as the man from Ernie's weighed Gram's fish, paid her, and pushed his way to his next customer.

"It was a good day." Gram pocketed her money and smiled at me. "Any errands you want to do before we go home?"

"Yes. I want to stop at a hardware store and buy a screwdriver and a bolt for the inside of my door."

After some chowder at Allamanda House, Gram and I walked to the third floor. The door hinges to the storeroom squeaked like a rusty oarlock, and I flinched in spite of myself. But of course an unused door would creak and squeak! People seldom came up here. Gram snapped on a light and whisked out a dustcloth she had tucked into her apron pocket.

"At least I can dust things off tonight so you can sort them without getting dirty tomorrow," Gram said.

"We could start making a pile of things to be discarded," I suggested.

"And another pile of things to be saved," Gram said.

I knew by Gram's tone which pile was going to be largest. I sensed that she hated to see any of this collection go.

"We'll have to tote some boxes up here tomorrow," I said. "But I don't know how we'll ever get them back down those steep stairs."

"Jason will help," Gram said. "He promised he would."

Before many minutes passed I forgot my uneasiness and became intrigued by the treasures we were uncovering.

"Look at these, Allison." Gram held a cardboard folder of pictures toward me. "They're baluster patterns that were used on the old Bahamas' houses. One of these days we'll have a tour of the city and I'll point out some other Bahamas' houses to you. The fancy gingerbread on many of Key West's old houses was carved by ships' carpenters while they were at sea. Their designs were their signatures. Visiting kin could tell at a glance which houses had been built by their relatives just by looking at the balcony rails." Gram placed the folder of designs in a box.

"Gram!" I held up a leather-covered book. "Here's an old diary. Is it yours?"

Gram took the book and leafed through it. "Never saw it before. The name Murdock's scrawled in it. I can't place the name." She snapped the book shut. "I'll put it in the box. Maybe the museum will be interested in it."

I sighed and laughed. "I may be an old lady before we ever get these two rooms cleared out at the rate we're going."

Gram glanced at her watch. "You're just tired tonight. Tomorrow there'll be no fishing for you. I'll go out alone and you can stay here and sort. I'll check your sorting when I get home." Gram placed a few more items in the box, then she straightened up. "Let's give it up for now and go to bed."

I was more than ready to follow that suggestion. Leaving the storeroom, we climbed down the narrow steps. I said good night in the hall and walked on to my own door-way. To my dismay I realized that I had forgotten to lock my room before going upstairs. Opening my door gingerly, I reached inside, groped along the wall, and flicked the light switch. No light.

"Bulb must have burned out," I muttered. Leaving my door wide open so a dim bar of light from the hallway shone inside my room, I stepped to my desk and snapped the switch on my reading lamp. Nothing. In my nervousness I knocked a book onto the floor and jumped, startled at the crash it made.

Fear tightened my throat. I wanted to scream, yet I hated to appear foolish. Only children were afraid of the dark. I banged into a chair, knocking it over on my way to my bedside lamp, which didn't work either. At this point I hadn't really expected it to work. But now what? I felt as if I were in the House of Horrors at an amusement park. Only this wasn't an amusement park. Allamanda House was real. All at once a shadow darkened my doorway. Goose bumps rose on my arms.

"Troubles?" Jason asked, his voice low and soothing. "Something wrong? I thought I heard some banging about in here."

"Oh, Jason!" I stepped into the hallway and tried to compose myself. "None of my lights will work. Do you suppose something's wrong with the wiring? Or maybe it's a fuse."

"Let me get a flashlight," Jason said. "I'll take a look around."

I waited in the hallway until Jason went to his room at the head of the stairs, then returned with a flashlight. Fanning the yellow beam toward my desk, Jason strode across the room to the lamp, flicked the switch to no avail, then tightened the bulb in the socket. Light flooded the desk.

"Bulb must have worked loose," Jason said. "They do that sometimes."

I stood on a chair and tightened the bulb in the ceiling fixture. Again there was light. And the same thing was true of my bedside lamp.

"Rather strange that the bulbs would all work loose at the same time, don't you think?" I asked. "Someone's trying to frighten me away from here, Jason."

"Don't be silly." Jason tugged at his sweater sleeves and stood with his head turned away from me. "Who'd want to do that?"

"That's what I'd like to know," I said. "Who?" In a rush of words I told Jason of the warning soaped on my mirror the day before.

"Sounds like Vondetta's tricks to me," Jason said. "These are childish pranks, and Vondetta's the youngest one in the house. She tries to look like she's thirty, but she's just a teenager. And she probably hates the idea of finding new living quarters. Bunny has spoiled her."

"Jason, is Vondetta your — your girl friend? I mean, maybe since you took me out yesterday —"

"Maybe she's jealous?" Jason asked. "Could be. I'd hesitate to guess at how Vondetta's mind works. I've noticed that she's been giving me the big come-on lately, but she certainly isn't my girl friend. I've never taken her out. Are you going to speak to your grandmother about the lights?"

I hesitated. Then I made up my mind. "No. Not tonight, at least. You're right. These are childish pranks. I'll not let them frighten me. Thank you for helping out."

Jason took his cue and left me alone, and I promptly locked my door and installed the bolt I had purchased that afternoon. The wood in the doorjamb was hard, but I worked and struggled until I twisted the screws into place.

Once in bed I couldn't sleep. I wasn't hungry. But neither was I sleepy. My face burned from too much sun. After squirming and turning for a long time, I got up and slipped into jeans and a shirt. At first I thought about reading. But then I remembered the orchid Vondetta had picked for me when I arrived. I had always liked to paint flowers.

"I'll paint," I muttered to myself. "I'll paint by moonlight. The garden gate's locked and there'll be nobody up at this hour. Painting will help me relax."

After quietly gathering easel, canvas, and paints from the storage closet, I tucked the flashlight Jason had left in my room into my pocket. All lights were out upstairs and downstairs. I slipped soundlessly along the hallway, down the steps, and into the garden.

At first I was tempted to run right back to my room. If the garden was a shadowy tangle of vegetation by day, it was an eerie black jungle by night. Yet enticing smells lured me along the bricked path. Blossoms that had emitted no scent in the daylight wafted fragrance into the darkness. I didn't know what the blossoms were, but they helped make the garden seem less forbidding.

Although the moon was only half full, the garden was silvered with light. It was almost as bright as at noon. For the first time I saw great beauty in Gram's plantings at Allamanda House. I lost no time in setting up my easel near the orchid plants and readying my paints. I might be unable to finish a painting tonight, but at least I could block it in and get a good start on it. Perhaps the moon would be out again tomorrow night.

As I sketched and measured, I listened to the night sounds of the garden. Wind rustled the palm fronds, and breezes whispered through the fringed branches of an Australian pine. High overhead a night bird wailed like a baby crying a lonesome lament.

I didn't know how long I had been working at my easel before the unnerving sensation of being watched chilled me. I had heard nothing unusual. I had seen nothing to make me uneasy. Exotic fragrances still wafted through the garden. But I felt as if someone were watching me. I could sense a hate-filled gaze boring into my spine.

Determined to show no weakness or fear, I rose quietly, packed away my paints, and folded my easel. From the pocket of my jeans I pulled the flashlight that I had brought along but hadn't used.

Now I flashed the beam of light onto the path in front of me, fanning it this way and that until it caught a huge earthenware jar in its scope. Was someone hiding there? Vondetta? Boldly I approached the jar, flashed my light inside, and stifled a sigh of relief. Empty.

I began to shake off my fear. Nobody lived in Allamanda House except Gram's friends. And no strangers had access to the garden once Gram locked the gate for the night. I was being foolish. No one was watching me.

I flashed the light across the ground until the beam illuminated something white caught on a crown-of-thorns plant. Out of curiosity I stepped closer. I flashed the beam directly onto the plant, but it took me several moments to understand what I was seeing. My hand shook as I realized that someone had torn the picture Ryan had sketched of me — torn it in half and impaled the pieces on the prickly thorn plant.

Chapter Seven

I suppressed an urge to scream as I ran toward the house. When I reached the porch, I calmed myself enough to tiptoe to my room. One thought seared my brain: I must search the room. Someone might be hiding there.

Like a child afraid of the boogy man, I peered inside my closet, under my bed, beneath my desk. All was in order. I breathed easier as I bolted the door and prepared for bed once more.

Tomorrow I would leave this house. I would pack my things and take off. But no. That was impossible. Fear had muddled my thinking. I couldn't run off and leave Gram here alone. She was my family — the family I had come to help. She needed me.

For the first time I realized that the last trick — the torn picture on the thorn plant — had probably been put there for Gram's benefit. Gram was the one who spent her spare minutes strolling through her garden, checking this plant, pruning that shrub. Whoever had impaled the picture on the thorns could hardly have expected me to find it.

As I calmed down I felt ashamed. I remembered that my father had often said that much of the world's villainy came from childish callousness. Somehow the memory of his words comforted me. Hadn't all these tricks been childish — soap on a mirror, loosened lightbulbs, a torn picture?

Of course I had been frightened, but I hadn't been harmed. I guessed that Vondetta was the person responsible for my discomfort. Vondetta was not only losing a place to live but also was seeing Jason turn his attentions in another direction.

I pulled the bed covers up under my chin and tried to sleep. I would tell nobody about tonight's scare, I decided. I refused to give Vondetta the satisfaction of knowing that she had frightened me.

Just as I was dropping off to sleep, a tapping on the ceiling awakened me. It lasted only a few moments. I held my breath in the waiting silence. The tapping came again. I sighed and burrowed down into the covers. Vondetta could stay up all night tapping on my ceiling for all I cared. My door was locked and bolted. I was perfectly safe. And I was determined to let no more childish pranks disturb me.

It seemed that the tapping continued all night, but when I opened my eyes in the morning, the tapping was at my door.

"Who's there?" I called, slipping into a robe and sandals.

"It's Gilda."

I hurried to open the door. "What is it, Gilda?"

In her black coveralls and kerchief Gilda loomed like a thundercloud in my doorway.

"I've come to invite you to go sponging with me today," Gilda said. "The sea is calm and the sun's bright. It'll be a good day."

"I've promised Gram to work on the storerooms today," I said, torn between dull duty and a promising adventure. "What time did you plan to leave?"

"I usually go out all day, but I have to make some repairs on my skiff," Gilda replied. "Could you work in the storeroom this morning and then go out with me this afternoon?"

"That sounds great," I agreed.

"I'll meet you downstairs right after noon," Gilda said, her voice echoing up and down the hallway. "Glad you're going with me. Sometimes I get lonesome out there all alone."

81

Gilda had no more than left than I had misgivings. I remembered a newspaper account of a crewman on a shrimp boat who had been lost overboard. If that sort of accident could happen on a shrimp boat, how easily such a thing might happen on a smaller craft. I felt gooseflesh prickle on my arms. Maybe Vondetta wasn't the person trying to frighten me away from Allamanda House. Maybe Gilda was guilty. And maybe Gilda was through fooling with small pranks.

I felt trapped, but I refused to admit my fear by backing out of the sponging trip. I ate a quick breakfast with Gram and then went to the third floor. Once in the storeroom I opened the ventilation hatches and began searching for some clues as to what or who might have made the tapping noise that had bothered me in the night. I found nothing. It was a hopeless search. Gram and I had walked around in the dust yesterday evening, so it was impossible to spot clear footprints.

I forced the memory of yesterday's strange happenings from my mind and settled down to work. After an hour or so I heard Gram's car leave the house, and I felt sorry for her having to work so hard at fishing. I was glad I had come to help her with the house.

I tossed some newspapers and a gaudy vase wrapped in red foil and decorated with crude daisies in one corner. Then I began sorting through the contents of an old box. I worked until my back began to ache before I paused to rest.

"Allison?" Jason's deep voice called from below, and I stuck my head through the doorway to see what he wanted.

"Bunny asked me to bring you up some boxes. If I lift them up, can you reach them?"

"I think so, Jason. Let me try." Clinging to the stairway handrail, I leaned down to grasp the boxes.

"Thanks so much," I said. "The boxes will help me organize this operation."

To my surprise, Jason climbed the stairs, carrying with him an armload of ropes and straps. "Promised Bunny I'd help you a bit if I could," he said. "Maybe if we haul out some of the big pieces of furniture we'll feel as if we're accomplishing something."

"But how can we ever lift them?" I welcomed Jason's company. I had been dreading a morning alone in the storeroom.

"We'll balance the stuff a piece at a time in these straps, then lower each item down to the second-floor hallway with the ropes. It'll take both of us to bring it off without an accident. Let's start with a chair."

Jason's dark expression was unreadable as he attached the leather straps to an old rocker.

"Now, if you'll go downstairs, Allison, I'll lower this rocker to you. You just guide it, keep it from banging against the stairs or the wall."

I obeyed. I clung to the railing halfway up the stairs, holding on with one hand while I guided the chair with the other. It was only moments before I realized how vulnerable my position was. Should Jason release the rope, the heavy chair would knock me to the floor below as it came crashing down on top of me.

But nothing of the sort happened, and I felt guilty at having suspected that Jason might try to harm me. How was I going to manage? I must stop imagining that everyone was plotting against me.

Together Jason and I lowered six chairs and a drop-leaf table to the hallway. Then Jason carried them on down the outside stairs while I climbed back to the store-room and continued sorting the smaller items. I stacked books in one box and dishes in another. I shoved the trash to be discarded into a corner for Gram to look over.

Jason joined me and we worked in silence for many minutes. But it was a companionable silence and I felt at ease. As the morning wore on, the heat in the storeroom became intense.

"If you'll forgive me, I'll roll up my sleeves," Jason said, running a finger under the turtleneck collar of his cotton shirt.

"Why, go right ahead," I said, puzzled.

"The scars are unpleasant to look at," Jason said. "I hide them whenever I can."

I tried not to gasp. Jason's forearms were etched with ugly white grooves from elbow to wrist, and an angry red scar ran from high on his upper arm down to his elbow.

"Whatever happened to you?" I blurted the question before I realized that I was invading Jason's privacy. "I mean —"

"It's all right," Jason said, trying to put me at ease. "I was in a fight when I was a kid. As you can see, I got the worst end of it." He rubbed his hand over his nose and chin. "It's the scars that show all the time that really get me down. Usually I can keep my arms covered."

"The scar on your chin is hardly noticeable," I said. "And as for your nose — well, it just makes your face more interesting. It really does."

Jason shrugged and said no more, but I

felt ill at ease. Jason's discomfort embarrassed me, and I sensed that I dared offer no sympathy.

At last I looked at my watch. "Jason, I'm going to have to stop work now. Gilda will be waiting for me and I have to wash off some of this grime before I can go sponging. Thank you so much for your help. I'm sure Gram will appreciate it, too."

"I was glad to assist. Allison?" Jason paused, and I looked at him, waiting for him to continue.

"Allison, if you're free late this afternoon, I'd like to show you a bit of the island and take you out for dinner."

"Why, I'd love that, Jason. But I have no idea when Gilda comes in from sponging."

"She's usually here by four o'clock. We could catch the Conch train around five and see the high spots of interest from it."

"The conk train?" I asked. "What's that?"

Jason spelled the word "Conch." "But it's pronounced conk like a conk on the head," he said. "It's a tourist attraction, but it offers an interesting hour or so."

"Sounds great and I'll be delighted to go with you."

Jason left me at my doorway and I hurried inside to freshen up for my afternoon adventure. When I went downstairs, Gilda was waiting on the porch.

"Feel up to walking to the skiff?" Gilda asked, thrusting her hamlike hands deep into the pockets of her black coverall.

"How far is it?" I asked. "Where do you keep your boat?"

"It's in a marsh about a mile from here," Gilda said.

"Why not take my car and save some time?" I offered.

Gilda's ragged smile revealed that she welcomed the chance to ride.

As we pushed our way through the heat of a dense mangrove thicket toward Gilda's boat, I imagined Key West in the days when pirates inhabited its coves and inlets.

Suddenly Gilda splashed into knee-deep water, grabbed a submerged rope that I hadn't even seen, and pulled a small flat-bottom boat into view. She maneuvered the skiff into position so I could step aboard without wetting my feet.

I sat down in the stern of the boat, trying to ignore the fetid odor that thickened the air.

"Don't let the stench get you down," Gilda said, grinning. "It'll get worse before it gets better." Striding to the bow of the boat, Gilda threw a tarp back, revealing a small mound of sponges. As she had predicted, the smell all but overcame us.

Gilda began poling the boat toward deeper water, and fortunately the fetid odor diminished.

"Want me to help row?" I looked at Gilda's pole on which three prongs pointed skyward, and I wondered where the oars were.

Gilda shook her head. "I just pole her along." Gilda broke the rhythm of her poling long enough to hand me a bucket with a glass bottom.

"We stay in shallow water and this is what I use for spotting sponge beds. Hold it over the side and see what you can see."

Relieved to know that we would be in shallow water, I obeyed, submerging the bucket a few inches into the sea. When I peered through the glass, I gasped in amazement.

"Gilda! It's beautiful down there. What an assortment of fish and sea life!"

Gilda nodded. With strong, smooth strokes she poled the boat for over half an hour before she stopped and took the bucket from me. Peering through it for a moment, she pulled it in and poled a bit further. She peered through the bucket once again, then handed it back to me.

"Take a look now. Look at the very bottom. See them? Sponges."

I looked until I saw the brownish mounds Gilda was pointing out. "But how do you bring them up, Gilda?"

"With this." Gilda reversed her pole so that the three prongs pointed downward. She peered through the bucket once more. Then, kneeling on the bottom of the skiff, she jabbed the pole into the water.

When Gilda stood up to shake a sponge from her pronged pole, the accident took place so fast that I hardly realized what had happened. Somehow Gilda slipped and fell, and one sharp prong on the pole pierced her thigh. She cried out once and jerked the prong from her leg. Then, as she sprawled prone on the bottom of the boat, blood spurted from her wound.

Chapter Eight

It took me only a moment to grasp the seriousness of the situation. Spurting blood meant that an artery in Gilda's leg had been severed or punctured. What to do? Probing into the depths of my mind, I recalled a first-aid course I had taken years ago. A tourniquet was needed. I jerked the macrame belt from my waist and tied it around Gilda's leg between the wound and her heart. But Gilda had already fainted.

Grabbing the pole, I stood and began poling the skiff toward the distant shore. How far we had come! It seemed like a million miles at this point. I couldn't pole steadily. I had to stop at frequent intervals to loosen the tourniquet lest I shut off all blood circulation from Gilda's leg.

Like a leering enemy the sun pounded on my head. Steamy heat enveloped me. I fought nausea as I strained at the pole. After endless minutes I managed to reach the mangrove swamp close to the spot where the car was parked.

I hated leaving Gilda alone in the boat,

but I had to. There was no other way. Dashing to the car, I drove to the nearest telephone and called a hospital. Then I hurried back to Gilda, who lay limp and white in the skiff. I had done all I could. From now on Gilda's fate rested in the hands of professionals.

The next ten minutes seemed like ten hours, but at last sirens screamed and help arrived. Orderlies lifted Gilda onto a stretcher and eased her into the ambulance.

At the hospital I waited over an hour before an orderly wheeled Gilda from the emergency room to private quarters.

"Will she be all right?" I stopped a nurse who stepped from Gilda's room.

"She's coming around, miss," the nurse replied. "Her wound has been treated and she's regained consciousness. It's a good thing you were there when the accident happened. You saved her life, you know. Had she been alone she would have died from loss of blood."

Just then a doctor poked his head through the doorway to Gilda's room. "Allison Blue?"

I nodded.

"Come in a moment, please. She's calling for you."

I hurried to Gilda's bedside, but Gilda said nothing until the doctor and nurses left us alone.

"I feel so miserable," Gilda said, her dark eyes reluctantly meeting mine.

"You'll feel better soon." I smiled. "It was just a freak accident. The nurse said —"

"That isn't what I mean." Gilda's booming voice dropped to a whisper. "I owe you a great apology, Allison Blue. I've been petty and mean to you, and here you've saved my life. Why, if you hadn't been with me —"

"You haven't been mean to me," I said, "and I'm glad I was there when you needed me. Now you just relax and try to sleep."

"I wrote on your mirror," Gilda said, turning her head away from me. "I loosened the light bulbs. I tore your picture and stuck it on the thorn plant."

I was speechless. I wanted to stamp my foot, to shout, and rave. But Gilda seemed fragile and vulnerable as a china figurine as she lay on the hospital bed under the stark-white sheet.

"Why, Gilda?" I fought back all emotion from my voice. "Maybe I can understand if you explain why. Were you trying to frighten me because you know you'll lose your room at Allamanda House if I help Gram move out? That's silly reasoning. Gram's going to sell whether or not I help."

"You've guessed correctly," Gilda said, "and I'll admit it was bad thinking. But my feelings about Allamanda House and Bunny Blue run deep. Bunny's a Conch and I'm a Greek. It's that simple."

"I don't understand at all," I said. "A conch is a shellfish. A conch is a tourist train."

"And a Conch is a person born and raised in Key West," Gilda replied. "Oh, Bunny and I are friends. I like her as a person, as an individual, but I hate Conchs."

"You're making no sense, Gilda." I stepped from Gilda's bed. "Let me call a nurse."

Gilda lifted her hand, motioning me to stay with her.

"After you've listened to me, then you can call a nurse." Gilda cleared her throat. "In the early nineteen-hundreds Key West was the greatest sponge market in the world. But by then most of the sponges had been taken from the shallow waters in the area. My people, the Greeks, introduced diving gear with weighted boots so the spongers could work in deeper water. The Conchs claimed the Greek boots were damaging the sponge beds, ruining them, causing a blight on the sponges."

"Were they?" I asked, wondering what all this had to do with me.

"Maybe so, maybe not. But the Conch officials outlawed the weighted boots. The Greeks ignored the law. One night the Conchs slipped to the docks and burned all the Greek boats. Well, that did it. My parents were ruined. Their livelihood depended on their boat. My people left Key West and lived in poverty in Tarpon Springs."

"You remember all this?" I asked.

"Some of it is just family hearsay, I suppose," Gilda said. "I was too young to really remember. But the family tales were real to me. As soon as I was old enough, I moved back to Key West. I love this island. The time came when I met Bunny Blue and she gave me a home at Allamanda House."

"And you've taken advantage of her friendship for years," I said. "She's let you live at Allamanda House rent free for ages. She told me so."

Gilda lowered her gaze, refusing to meet

my eyes. "Bunny's a Conch, and I guess I just figured that because the Conchs had destroyed my family's boats, they owed me something. I'll admit that I've taken advantage of Bunny. But she allowed it. She's soft. You know she's a real marshmallow of a woman. Your arrival brought things to a head. I knew I was going to have to find another place to live."

"Having to move is your own fault," I said. "Gram can't support Allamanda House when she has hardly any money coming in. Of course, if everyone began paying his fair share . . ."

I waited for Gilda to agree to pay her rent, but the words did not come. An awkward silence mushroomed between us until I felt obliged to speak.

"Don't you worry any more about these things right now, Gilda. Just concentrate on getting well. And forget about trying to frighten me. I can understand your feelings and I appreciate your telling me and easing my mind. Your pranks were harmless, but I'll admit that I was scared. And I'll also admit that the tapping on my ceiling was really getting on my nerves."

"Tapping?" Gilda raised her eyebrows. "I wasn't doing any tapping, Allison. Just the three things I mentioned. Are you going to tell Bunny on me?"

I smiled to myself at the thought of this big, strapping woman worrying like a child about whether or not I was going to tell on her.

"Wouldn't you rather tell Gram yourself?" I asked.

Gilda scowled and nodded. "Yes — I'll tell her. That's the least I can do. I know she must be concerned about your safety. I'll tell her. And I promise you — no more tricks."

I reached over and squeezed Gilda's hand just as the nurse came in and asked me to leave the room.

"Good-bye, Gilda," I called. "I'll see you later. I think we've both learned a lot this afternoon."

I drove home slowly, my mind reeling with all that had happened. I felt guilty because mentally I had blamed Vondetta for trying to frighten me. Now I knew that childish callowness could be perpetrated by adults as well as by young people. One did not necessarily grow wiser just because one grew older.

So much had happened that it seemed much later than half past three. I shook my watch and held it to my ear. It was ticking. I showered, and with a fear-free mind I lay down for a nap before meeting Jason for our afternoon date.

No more than a half hour passed, but I awakened feeling refreshed and eager to ride the Conch train. I wrote a brief note to Gram telling her about Gilda. When I strolled downstairs to leave the note in the kitchen where Gram would be sure to see it, Jason was waiting for me in an easy chair on the porch.

Jason stood, a slight smile playing on his lips. "How was sponging?"

"Jason! It was just awful." I poured out the story of my afternoon, but I omitted telling of Gilda's confession. Jason would hear of that only if Gilda wanted him to hear.

"I've often thought that Gilda was foolish to go out sponging alone," Jason said. "The sea can be treacherous, and an emergency situation can arise in a matter of seconds."

I stepped inside the house long enough to leave the message on the kitchen table. Then Jason and I drove to Front Street where the Conch train stopped. Jason purchased tickets, and within ten minutes the black and yellow train with its make-believe engine stopped at the passenger-loading zone.

"Let's ride in the last car," Jason said, helping me onto a seat.

The sun was shining brightly, and I was thankful for the yellow and black canopy that shaded our car. Jason placed his arm on the back of the seat behind us, lightly touching my shoulder. I relaxed. I was ready to enjoy our trip.

"There's Hemingway's old house up ahead," Jason said before the guide could announce it. "Writers like this island. I guess it gives them the sense of isolation that they need for indulging in creative work."

"I wish I knew about these palms," I said. "There are so many different kinds. They're all similar in nature, yet each one is unique. I'd like to paint them all."

"The one straight ahead and to our right is a no-trespassing palm," Jason said. "See? The name's right on it."

As we passed the tree I saw a "No Trespassing" sign that someone had posted to protect his property. I grinned at Jason's humor. For the next few moments Jason was silent as our guide pointed out cork trees, rubber trees, papaya trees, and a traveler's palm.

Jason nodded to our right. "About five miles out in the Atlantic there's a coral reef

— the only one in the continental United States. In the early eighteen-hundreds the reef caused a lot of shipwrecks. For a long time many Key Westers made their living from the sale of salvage from wrecks. Some of the sea captains were extremely wealthy."

"Gram mentioned that to me," I said. "That sounds like a grim way to make a living."

"But it was a fact. When a wreck was sighted, the first ship captain to reach it could claim the salvage. That was the law. And that's why Allamanda House as well as a few other old homes here have a widow's walk on the roof. The sea captains paced those lofty walks day and night trying to be the first to sight a wreck. The salvage business ended when the Key West lighthouse came into operation and when steamboats replaced the sailing vessels."

I would much rather have listened to Jason than to the tour guide. An hour or so later when the Conch train carried us back to our starting point, I felt as if I knew a lot about the island. I could easily understand why Gram had been content to live her life here, and I wondered why my father had felt he must leave. But I didn't dwell on that thought. My father had done what he had to do. He had seen a need and he had tried to fill it.

"Where would you like to eat?" Jason asked as we strolled back toward Front Street.

"You pick the place," I said. "You know what's good."

"Then let's try Sloppy Joe's. It's a cafe where Hemingway liked to hang out. But more important, they serve excellent seafood there."

Jason linked his arm through mine and we strolled several blocks through the soft twilight to Sloppy Joe's. From the outside the cafe looked like nothing special. But once we were inside and my eyes adjusted to the dimness, I began to absorb the special atmosphere.

Opened parachutes covered the ceiling of the cafe, and on one wall blue sailfish hung on either side of a huge picture of Ernest Hemingway. Paintings offered for sale by local artists were on another wall, and I studied them and inhaled the enticing aroma of chowder while Jason placed our order.

"We're early," Jason said. "Most people won't come in until much later in the evening. We'll have the place pretty much to ourselves. I like it that way." Jason touched the hump on his nose and I sighed.

"You shouldn't be so sensitive, Jason. I insist that your nose makes your face handsome, unique."

"It makes me angry and bitter." Jason wedged the words between clenched teeth. "If I had been beaten in an ordinary fight I might have been able to face my defeat. But my father did this to me, Allison. My own father. He was nothing but a drunken gambler. And when he was drunk he was dangerous."

If I could have thought of anything to say, I would have interrupted Jason. But his eyes held mine in a hypnotic gaze. I couldn't break away, nor could I find words to stop him.

"One night my father came in fairly loaded and he began picking on my mother. How she ever tolerated her marriage to him is more than I'll ever understand. But this night he was violent and mean. He slapped Mom and I dashed to her rescue. I was ten at the time."

I said nothing. Jason seemed to be talking more to himself than to me, and I hesitated to interrupt.

"I used to haye a diary of my grandmother's that told a lot about my mother, but somehow I misplaced it. I wish I had it back. Mother was a good woman, but Dad was so mean he overshadows her in my memory. How I remember him! I was ten years old at the time of the beating. I was protecting my mother. I flung myself against my father. I can still feel the way his metal overall buttons cut into my face. Strange that I should remember that when I really don't remember the pain of my injuries."

"Maybe there are some things that we are mercifully allowed to forget," I said.

"My father almost killed me that night, Allison. Afterward I was in the charity ward of a hospital for months, and I've spent the rest of my life maimed and scarred. But I won't let my beating be for nothing. I'm going to prove to the world that I'm a better man than my father was. I've got an education. I've got hard-earned money that I've saved and invested. And I'll soon have Allamanda House."

"I understand," I said. "I really do." I knew it was useless to tell Jason that his scars didn't matter, useless to suggest the possibility of cosmetic surgery. I guessed now that Jason's mind was almost as badly scarred as his body. My heart ached for him, and impulsively I leaned toward him and kissed him.

Chapter Nine

I lay awake a long time that night, and when I did doze it seemed that I was awakened almost immediately. Someone was upstairs in the storeroom. Footsteps made the floorboards creak. The strange tapping that I had heard before was repeated at intervals as I listened, puzzled.

It couldn't be Gilda. She was in the hospital. She had admitted her pranks and she had denied the tapping. Rising from bed, I decided to find out just what was going on upstairs.

I slipped into my robe. But as I was feeling about on the floor for my sandals, I knocked my alarm clock over. To my dismay the alarm began ringing, and it took me several moments to get it stopped. I held my breath, listening. The tapping sounded again.

Without bothering with shoes, I slipped into the hall and tiptoed to the stairs. Some of the steps squeaked, but I eased myself to the third floor as quietly as I could. Squeezing by the stair banister, I peered into the room on my left. All was quiet. The moonlight shining through the window revealed an almost empty room. I moved to the closet and looked inside. Empty. I breathed easier.

Going to the room at the right of the stairway, I snapped on the light. Except for the objects we were packing away, the room was deserted. And the closet was empty.

I felt quite foolish as I climbed back downstairs and returned to my room. But again I bolted my door and turned the key in the lock. I knew I had not imagined the tapping on my ceiling. Someone had been on the third floor only a few minutes ago. My jangling alarm clock had probably frightened them away. But away to where? Surely I would have heard anyone who came down the stairway into the hall.

I slept restlessly the remainder of the night.

For the rest of the weekend Jason and I worked hard in the storerooms, and once school started on Monday I missed his help. But our hard work had paid off. By Monday evening both third-floor rooms stood empty. During the weekend Gram had sold the furniture, given it away, or moved it to other rooms.

On Tuesday morning I dressed and walked down to the lower porch, where I was dismayed to find Gram sitting on the swing, crying. She made no sound, but tears coursed down her weathered cheeks.

"Gram! Whatever is the matter?"

"I'm all right," Gram said, wiping her eyes. "But I won't say I feel fine. I have an appointment today that I'm dreading. It's — it's the beginning of the end, Allison. Allamanda House will soon belong to someone else."

"Gram! You really hate the idea of selling, don't you?"

"Yes. Yes, I really do. This is my home."

"You don't have to leave here unless you want to. Surely you know that."

"But we've done all that work," Gram said. "You've come all this way and taken vacation time to help me."

"That doesn't matter, Gram. I came to Key West because I wanted to. I wanted to be with my family. I've only helped you get ready to sell because I thought selling was what you wanted. There's no reason why you can't change your mind and keep Allamanda House. You've made no actual promise to Jason nor to anyone else, and you've signed no papers."

"There's the matter of money," Gram said. "I simply can't afford Allamanda House."

"You can afford it if you want to afford it," I said, exasperation creeping into my voice. "All you would have to do to keep Allamanda House is to put it on a paying basis. Rent those two extra rooms we've just cleared out and tell your freeloading pals to pay up or get out. Get a little starch in your spine, Gram."

"Oh, Allison, I couldn't just up and demand money from my friends. What would they think of me?"

I stood and glared at Gram. "You're saying that you'd rather turn your friends out of their rooms than give them the opportunity to assume the financial responsibility that is rightfully theirs. Look at it that way. Give your friends a chance to do the right thing. They can't read your mind. You'll have to speak out. Maybe they'd rather pay up than move."

"I can't do it, Allison. I can't just all of a sudden demand money from these people."

"You'll have to, Gram. If you really want to keep Allamanda House, you have no other choice. It's a hard decision to make, and of course Vondetta and Gilda and maybe even Ryan will fuss, but . . ." I paused a moment, thinking of my own decision to leave Ron in New York. "Gram, no positive action will meet with universal approval. Only an amoeba can look like a nice guy to everyone."

"I know you're right." Gram wiped her tears away. "But I — just can't — do it."

"Then with your permission I'll do it for you. Would that make it easier? I'm not as close to your so-called friends as you are. I can deliver the message loud and clear."

"Allison! I'd be ever so grateful if you'd tell them."

"I'll do it right after dinner," I said.

"What about Jason?" Gram asked. "He'll be more affected by this decision than the rest of them. I really hate to disappoint him."

"Jason will survive," I said. "There are other Bahamas' houses on the island that he can buy and restore. He doesn't have to have Allamanda House to make his dream of owning a showplace come true. But he really does deserve to know of your decision ahead of the others. I'll call him at school."

"Yes, Allison. That would be the thing to do. If you'll take care of that, I'll cancel my appointment with my lawyer."

I felt a surge of excitement at the change

in plans that had happened so quickly. I would place an advertisement in the newspaper for the two third-floor rooms. But first things first. I went to the telephone and dialed the high school.

"May I speak to Jason McKillum?" I asked when the secretary answered.

"I'm sorry," the secretary replied. "Mr. McKillum has a class right now. May I take a message?"

"Yes," I replied. "Have him call Miss Allison Blue at his first opportunity. It's most important."

After I replaced the receiver I hurried to the kitchen and began helping Gram prepare lunch.

A few minutes after lunchtime I excused myself from the kitchen and went to my room to think. Jason hadn't returned my call, and I kept one ear tuned for the ring of the telephone. But I needed to be alone, to plan my exact words. I knew my message to the roomers at Allamanda House was going to be unpopular, so I wanted to phrase it as diplomatically as possible. Sitting at my desk, I jotted notes, discarded them, then muttered aloud to the four walls.

That night at dinner, everyone was present at the table except Jason. The fact that he hadn't returned my call nagged at my mind. There would be no time now to speak to him ahead of time.

Although the food tasted delicious, tension gripped the room. I sensed that everyone was on guard, looking at his neighbor from the corner of his eye. As soon as Gram poured coffee, I rose.

The guests snapped to attention as if I had sounded a trumpet fanfare. My tongue felt dry as a cotton swab, but I managed to speak.

"A few days ago my grandmother surprised you with her plans to sell Allamanda House. I am happy to announce that those plans have been changed. Allamanda House will not be sold. Grandmother and I hate to disappoint Jason, but we feel that he can buy and restore some other Bahamas' house. All of you may retain your rooms here — if you pay your rent on a regular basis. I mean this. It is important. Gram can no longer support Allamanda House without the aid of regular rent payments. This should come as no shock to you."

In the silence that followed my announcement, I felt eyes boring into my back. I whirled around to face Jason. The color had drained from his face. I knew that he had heard my announcement, had heard it with no forewarning.

"Jason!" Gram exclaimed. "Do join us for coffee."

"I tried to call you," I said. "Didn't the school secretary deliver my message?"

Jason nodded. "I got it. You said that it was urgent that you talk to me, so I thought we could talk more privately in person than over the telephone."

"Oh, Jason!"

"This whole thing's unfair," Vondetta said as her mind absorbed the import of my announcement.

Jason's arrival had upset me so that I could hardly collect my thoughts. Jason deserved better than this. If only he had called me as I had requested!

"It's unfair." Vondetta's voice demanded my attention, and somehow I found words to answer her.

"The decision to stay at Allamanda House or to leave is an individual matter," I said. "Tomorrow is rent-collection day. Anyone not paying his room rent retroactive to the first of the month will have to find other living quarters immediately. I'm sorry, but there can be no exceptions."

My knees were shaking so badly that I was glad to sit down. I was unprepared for the storm of words that flooded the room.

"I've lived here for months with no trouble until you came nosing around." Vondetta glared at me.

"Maybe you should find another place to live," Gilda shouted at Vondetta. "There are plenty of other rooming houses on this island."

I grinned at Gilda, welcoming her unexpected support.

"You've hated me from the day we met," Vondetta said to me, ignoring Gilda's remarks.

"There is nothing personal about this change in plans and in management," I said. "It is a matter that should have been taken care of ages ago."

"I'll pay my rent for this month right now," Gilda announced, "and I'll make up back payments as I'm able to."

"I appreciate that, Gilda," Gram said. "I do appreciate it."

Gilda blushed. "I've been meaning to do it ever since . . ." Gilda's voice trailed off and then she met my gaze. "I think it's time the Conchs and the Greeks declared a truce."

"What do you mean?" Gram stared at Gilda, but I winked in understanding. Before either of them could speak again,

Jason's glare darkened the room. He scraped his chair back from the table.

"I've always paid my rent," Jason said. "And I resent being grouped with these — these deadbeats."

Ryan leaped up so quickly that I thought he was going to punch Jason, but instead Ryan reached into his pocket for his checkbook.

"I'm paying right now," Ryan said. "And I suggest that you do likewise, Vondetta. We've taken unfair advantage of Bunny. Allison's right. It has to stop."

Vondetta rose and flounced from the room with Jason following at her heels.

Chapter Ten

Tactfully Gilda began clearing the table, and I spoke to Ryan.

"Thanks for backing us up, Ryan. But Gram didn't mean for you to start paying rent. Your trading rent payments for fishing fees is all that has kept Allamanda House going this long."

"Let Ryan pay," Gram said, patting a fluff of gray hair that hung over one ear. "I've gone fishing for the last time — commercially, that is. I think your plan's going to work, Allison. Vondetta may gripe and complain, but I believe she'd rather pay than move."

"I hope you're right," I said. "But if she doesn't pay and if Gilda backslides, you can always advertise for new tenants. It's time you began looking after your own interests."

Before I quite knew what had happened, Gram had joined Gilda in the kitchen and I was left alone with Ryan.

"I really admired you," Ryan said. "That was a nasty chore to be stuck with. You have more spunk than I've been giving you credit for. I think we've all mistakenly gone on the assumption that Bunny was independently wealthy. In fact, I believe she intended for us to believe that."

"I'm sure she did," I said. "In her own way she was trying to repay a favor that — someone did for her. Her motives were good, but her method was impractical."

"Bunny always let on that her fishing was pure pleasure," Ryan said, shaking his head. "Once Vondetta gets used to the idea that Bunny needs the money to keep Allamanda House in the black, I think she'll come across with no hard feelings. Bunny has really been like a mother to us all."

"I'm worried about Jason," I said. "I wanted to tell him privately that Gram had decided not to sell. I called the school and left a message for him to call me. Instead he just dropped by in person."

"He'll get over it." Ryan snorted. "I did. I thought Allamanda House might belong to me until Jason overbid me. I was disappointed, but I survived. I even thought that at some later time when my financial situation was more stable I might be able to persuade Jason to resell to me."

"Why did you want the house?" I asked.

"To live in, why else? I think it would

make a great family home. Why do you suppose Jason's so eager to own the place?"

"Because of its historical importance," I said. "Jason told me he planned to restore Allamanda House, to turn it into an exhibition place. He loves history, Ryan. Why, he knows more Key West lore than the tour guides on the Conch trains. I can understand why Allamanda House attracts him. There aren't too many houses on the island that still have a widow's walk perched on the roof."

"Somehow I can't believe that Jason wants Allamanda House just for its historical value," Ryan said. "Jason's a strange one. As long as I've known him, he's worked every spare minute of his life and lived like a miser. I could hardly believe it when I learned that all his scrimping, saving, and slaving had been in an effort to accumulate money to buy Allamanda House. I think he was planning to fix the place up and resell at a huge profit. Jason's after the dollar."

"I doubt that," I said.

"Something about the whole setup rings false. For a time I felt confident that eventually I could buy this place if Jason bought it first. Of course, I realized that I'd have to name the right price. Why would a person sacrifice his very life for an old run-down house unless he thought he could turn a nice profit?"

"I've no idea," I said. "But you're making me feel terrible about this. I didn't know all these things about Jason. How I wish I had been able to speak to him in private, to prepare him for the change in plans! In a way I can understand him, Ryan. When a person wants something badly enough, he'll do almost anything to get it."

"You're speaking from personal experience?" Ryan led the way to the porch, and I followed him to the swing where we sat down.

I laughed at Ryan's question. "Well, for two years I've pinched pennies hoping I could go off somewhere alone and try my hand at being a creative painter instead of a commercial artist. I have a while to work yet, though."

Ryan grinned at me. "I can make your dream come true for a few hours at least. I have tomorrow off. Let's spend the afternoon painting. Where would you like to go?"

For an instant I felt the barrier between myself and Ryan disappear. It was as if we were friends of long standing. My memory of a frightening sea captain with a rifle disappeared as Ryan grinned at me like a small boy eager to be off on a picnic. I leaped at the chance to join him.

"I told you that I like to paint scenes that are unique," I said. "How about going to the city cemetery?"

Ryan blinked in surprise. "Ah! A real romantic. I make a date with a beautiful girl and she asks me to go to the cemetery."

"If you don't like that idea, we could go to Key West Bight. I'd like to paint a shrimp boat, but I'm afraid to go there alone. It's such a busy place. I might get in somebody's way."

Ryan grinned again. "Those shrimpers are too smelly for my preference. I vote for the cemetery. I'll have to agree with you that it's unique."

The next day after lunch I hurried out to the kitchen to tell Gram of our plans.

"Better leave your heart here with me," Gram said. "I'm afraid you'll fall and break it."

"Gram!" I felt my face flush. "We're just going painting."

"Just going painting." I knew there was more to our outing than that because my hands shook as I stacked a few dishes in the cupboard. Yet why shouldn't I be keyed up and nervous after all I had been through the day before?

"I'm just joking, Allison," Gram said. "But do remember that tonight my committee is scheduled to work at the museum. Eight o'clock."

"I'd almost forgotten," I admitted. "Who's on your committee?"

"Just the people here at Allamanda House," Gram said. "My friends. At least I hope they're still my friends. You'll be back in time, won't you?"

"Sure thing, Gram. I'm looking forward to actually seeing that museum. See you later."

Leaving Gram, I hurried to the second-floor storage closet for my paint supplies. Although I offered my car for the afternoon, Ryan insisted that we take his truck. Its bulk almost filled the narrow street that led to the cemetery in the old part of town.

"Just what is there here that attracts you so?" Ryan asked as he drove through the gateway to the cemetery.

"Hi, there, Ryan," a man called from where he stood waist deep in a freshly dug grave.

"Good afternoon, Ben," Ryan called.

"How's it going?" Ryan waved and drove on.

"The graves attract me for one thing," I said once I had Ryan's attention again. "So many seem to be encased in cement vaults above the ground."

"And for good reason," Ryan said. "You can't dig very deep in this area without hitting water." He parked his truck under a date palm, and we walked along a path where coarse grass pushed up through loose gravel.

I lugged my easel and paints past many family plots that were enclosed by concrete block walls about three feet high with wrought-iron gates. In some places palm trees waved above tall grave markers, silvered urns, and plaster statues of the Virgin Mary.

"Look at this." I stopped at a neatly fenced plot. "This whole area is paved with brick."

"Makes upkeep easier," Ryan said. "Some of these plots that may seem to have been abandoned really have not been. Plant growth is so rapid in this warm climate that it quickly gets out of control."

"Ryan, look!" I pointed to a bouquet of hibiscus that decorated an old grave. "That vase!"

"What about it?" Ryan asked. "That's probably a Spanish plot. Cuban families frequently use brightly colored ornaments on their family graves."

"That's not what I mean," I said. "That vase came from Allamanda House. That red foil, those daisies around the rim. I'd recognize it anywhere."

"Are you sure?" Ryan asked.

"Positive. I found it while I was cleaning out those upstairs storerooms. We discarded it. Strange that it should turn up here."

"Abbie Murdock." Ryan read the inscription on the grave marker. "Never heard of that name before. Someone probably just filched the vase from a trash dump, found it handy, and used it."

I forgot about the vase as I set my easel before a large, well-kept plot of ground that was enclosed by a spiked fence. "This is what I'm going to paint, Ryan. That statue."

"It's a memorial to the victims of the disaster of the U.S. battleship *Maine* in Havana Harbor February fifteenth, eighteen ninety-nine," Ryan said, reading part of the inscription from the marker. "While you work here, I'm going over to the edge of the cemetery and try to paint a likeness of that graceful Australian pine."

"Fine." I put on a large-brimmed hat to shade my eyes and face from the sun before I began working. Indeed, I had found a unique spot. A few blocks to my right the Gulf of Mexico gleamed in the sunlight, and a few blocks to my left the Atlantic Ocean pounded the shore. I tried to capture the romance of my location on canvas, hoping that I was unlike the average tourist who saw only the surface of the scenes he visited.

It was almost four hours later when I sensed someone peering over my shoulder. I had been so absorbed in my work that I had all but forgotten about Ryan.

"You truly are an artist, Allison," Ryan said, admiring my painting. He showed me his picture of the pine, and I was equally complimentary about his work.

"We should form a mutual admiration society," I said, laughing. "But at least you know now why I'd like very much to give up commercial art."

"I'm afraid that anyone who hopes to make a living by painting is in for a disappointment," Ryan said. "Even the big-name artists sometimes have a rough go of it. I want to show you something, Allison. Do you have to be home at any special time?"

I nodded. "By eight o'clock. This is

Gram's night to work at the museum. Aren't you one of her committee?"

"Right." Ryan grinned. "Glad you reminded me. The museum is a worthy project. Lots of people donate a few spare hours to its maintenance. But let's pack up and leave this spot for now. We can come back another day."

We carried our things to the truck. Then Ryan drove to a fabric shop. "I want to show you this place. It's arranged so people can watch the hand-screening process."

I let Ryan lead the way into the rear entrance of a long, narrow building.

"*Buenos dias,* Senor Bell." A Cuban worker looked up from his job and smiled and waved. Then he turned his attention back to the chore at hand. He and his partner mixed paints, poured them into a framed screen, and applied the design to yards of fabric that were stretched on tables the length of the building. Inhaling the paint smell, I watched for many moments before I spoke.

"It's all very interesting, Ryan."

"The most interesting thing to you might be that this business hires artists to create the designs they use on the fabrics. You might want to check into that sometime."

I smiled. "Perhaps. But for now Acme Advertising awaits me in Miami."

Ryan took me to a sidewalk cafe that was ringed with blooming hibiscus and shaded in part by a huge banyan tree. As we lingered over our meal, I confided in Ryan.

"You know, this is the first time that I've really felt completely at ease with you. The barrier is gone."

"What barrier?" Ryan gazed into the distance where the waters of the bay gleamed in the sunlight.

"The barrier you erect between yourself and the people you don't really want to know too well. Don't think I haven't felt it these days I've been at Allamanda House. You have loads of friends. People greet you from every side, yet I sense that few people know you well. You have a way of retreating into yourself."

The breeze wafted through the banyan leaves for several moments before Ryan answered.

"Once a fellow's been hurt, he learns to create protective devices to prevent himself from being hurt again." Ryan stood and waited at my elbow until I rose. Then he led the way from the restaurant, heading across the street toward Mallory Dock.

As we strolled beside the water, I inhaled

the scent of the trade wind. It was like a heady perfume, and something in it gave me the courage to ask the question I had been wondering about.

"Ryan, Gram told me that you were soured on girls. Why?"

Ryan paused for so long that I wished I had kept my mouth shut.

"Hasn't Vondetta told you?" Ryan asked bitterly. "When a guy gets jilted, he's seldom happy about it. Vondetta and I had planned to be married in the spring. Then, suddenly and with no explanation, Vondetta changed her mind, returned my ring, and started chasing Jason."

Vondetta! For a moment I was stunned to think that Ryan would fall for a girl like Vondetta. Then I sighed. Vondetta was undeniably pretty, and she could be winsome and charming when she wanted to be.

"I'm sorry, Ryan. I had no right to pry into your private affairs."

"Don't be sorry. I lived on self-pity for a while, but I'm over that now. Vondetta is a girl of the past as far as I'm concerned."

I wondered if Ryan's words were true. As I stood there by the sea, Ryan took me in his arms and kissed me. Almost immediately I was kissing him back with a warmth that surprised me.

Chapter Eleven

To my dismay Ryan drove me back to Allamanda House almost immediately. I tried to talk to him during the ride, but he had thrust the invisible shield between us again. The shield was nothing I could see or touch, but I sensed its presence and felt chilled. Ryan Bell had a hard core that frightened me.

I was glad that Gram was still sitting on the front porch when Ryan and I arrived home. A third person lessened the tension between us. I excused myself from Ryan and joined Gram.

"Have a good time?" Gram asked.

"I thought we were having a good time," I said. "But all of a sudden — poof. Ryan turned off the charm and began treating me as if I were his worst enemy."

"I warned you," Gram replied.

"Why didn't you tell me that Vondetta was the girl who jilted Ryan?"

"You didn't ask." Gram sighed. "Forget Ryan, Allison. What's happened between you and Jason? I had the idea that you two were kindling a warm friendship."

Jason. Again I felt chilled. Jason was angry at me and so was Ryan. But at least I still had a chance to apologize to Jason.

"Is Jason in?" I parried Gram's question with one of my own.

"As far as I know he is," Gram replied. "He's planning to go with us to the museum. You hadn't forgotten, had you?"

"I hadn't forgotten," I said. "I guess I can talk to Jason at the museum. Think I'll run upstairs and slip into some work clothes."

"Allison, how can I ever thank you for taking a stand for me on the rent payments?"

"Forget it, Gram. Anyway, you have no idea how much good it did. Only time will tell." I stood up. "Be back in a jiffy."

I was only a few moments in changing my clothes. But when I returned to the lower porch, everyone was waiting for me. Vondetta and Gram carried hangers of freshly pressed costumes. Gilda carried a basket loaded with furniture polish and soft rags, and Jason and Ryan carried window-cleaning equipment. Gram's ability to organize this crew of people into a temporary work force amazed me. And if they resented her decision to get tough about rent collection, they didn't show it. Even Vondetta seemed eager to help.

"We'd better take two cars," Gram said. "I don't want to be so crowded that we wrinkle these costumes that I've spent all afternoon laundering and ironing. I'll drive my car. Vondetta, you ride with me and help hold the costumes."

"I'll ride with you, too, Bunny," Gilda said. "It's hard for me to fold my long legs into that Volkswagen of Allison's."

"I'll drive the truck," Ryan said. "Forget the VW. We can stow our cleaning equipment in the back end of the pickup."

We walked single file through the dank-smelling garden, and I followed the group to the curbing where the cars were parked. As I started to get in Gram's car, Gilda stopped me.

"You ride with Ryan, Allison. These costumes need to be spread flat on the back seat."

"Come on," Jason called. "There's plenty of room for three in the cab of the truck."

Reluctantly I followed Jason to the truck and slid onto the seat between him and Ryan. Ryan sat there like a robot performing the mechanics of driving. Nobody spoke on the brief ride to the museum. I could sense anger surrounding me, but I could do little about it. I had nothing to say to Ryan, and I certainly wasn't going to apologize to Jason about Allamanda House with Ryan right there listening to every word. What an unfortunate night for a clean-up party. Everyone was angry with everyone else, yet everyone was determined to carry on as if nothing were wrong.

When we reached the museum, Jason unlocked the door with his custodian's key and pulled a master switch that turned on the lights. For once Gram asserted herself and gave us our instructions.

"Gilda, you help Vondetta carry the costumes down this long hallway to the period rooms and I'll join you there in a few moments."

"There isn't room for three of us to work in those tiny rooms," Vondetta complained.

"You and I will dress the figures as we usually do," Gram said. "Gilda will polish furniture. She's only going to help carry the costumes while I show Allison the chore I have in mind for her."

"Ryan and I will begin polishing the glass display cases," Jason said. "Right?"

"Right." Gram nodded, then smiled at

me. "Come along, Allison. I'll let you work in the art exhibit rooms." She handed me a soft cloth. "It won't be hard work, but it will take some time. I want you to dust all the picture frames."

Within minutes we were all at our tasks, and I was thoroughly enjoying mine. I had a chance to study each picture as I worked. Sometimes I had to stand on a step stool to reach the tops of the frames, but for the most part the work was as easy as Gram had said it would be.

I could hear the others moving about as they worked, and time passed quickly. When I finished dusting the last frame in the third exhibit room, I wandered down a hallway, studying the old fortress carefully for the first time.

In the center of the structure was a large room with solid masonry walls, Romanesque arches, and a high platform where cannons could be mounted. A plaque explained that this part of the museum, which used to be a fortress, was called the citadel, a place to which the defenders could fall back in case they could hold the ramparts no longer.

I felt guilty wandering about while the others were still working, but curiosity urged me on. I could hear Ryan whistling as he polished a glass display case, and a glance over my shoulder told me that Jason was repairing a damaged wall plaque. I wouldn't be missed for a few moments.

A cistern and a fireplace had been built into the citadel so the troops could have water and heat and so they could cook even though they might be under seige. A short distance beyond the citadel I came to another plaque near the entryway to the tower of the fortress.

I snapped on a light that illumined both the plaque and the foot of a circular stairway. This plaque warned the tourist that he explored this section of the fort at his own risk, and it warned all children to be accompanied by an adult.

Hesitating only a moment, I mounted the stairs that wound upward like a corkscrew. The steps, wide at the wall and tapering to nothing at the unprotected side, were made of metal, and my shoes clanged against them, making them ring as I walked. No handrail offered safety or support, but I pressed against the earthy-smelling wall and eased upward step by step. Light from the bulb in the lower entryway diminished as I ascended until I was climbing in almost total darkness.

How high? A hundred feet — perhaps

more. I couldn't guess. Common sense advised me to go back down, but my artist's eye demanded to see the view from the top of the tower. I eased on upward until I stepped outdoors onto a moonlit vantage spot. But still I was not at the fortress's highest point. Outside the tower proper I found a few more stairs leading to a small observation platform. Here there was a handrail, and I hurried up these last few steps.

I felt as if I were standing in the clouds and peering down upon a miniature world below me. To my right huge beacons lighted the airport landing strip, while to my left moonlight shimmered on the undulating sea. Surely, I thought, I must come up here one day before my vacation ended and paint. But that day would have to be soon.

As I stood facing into the salty trade wind, the drone of an airplane masked the pounding of the surf against the sea wall. I watched as a small air taxi touched down on a concrete runway flanked by salt pools. I was so engrossed in the pilot's smooth landing that it was a moment or so before I realized that the car that had just pulled onto the highway below me was Gram's.

Surely she wouldn't leave without me!

"Gram! Vondetta!" Rushing to the railing around the observation platform, I shouted at the departing car. But how foolish! Gram couldn't hear me. Anyway, I had ridden here with Ryan. Gram probably assumed that I would be returning to Allamanda House with him.

Not wanting to keep Ryan or Jason waiting, I hurried down from the lookout and slipped inside the tower onto the circular stairs.

"Jason!" I shouted down the cylinder of steps, and my voice echoed into blackness. "Jason, I'll be right there."

I wanted to hurry, but in the pitch darkness I could only inch slowly from one step to the next. I had expected this darkness, for I remembered that when I climbed up here, light near the top exit was almost nonexistent. But as I eased on downward, I did not seem to be coming any nearer to the light I had turned on at the foot of the steps. I started to panic only when I heard Ryan's truck motor starting.

They were leaving me! For a moment I made a frantic effort to climb back to the lookout. But as one foot slipped off the narrow wedge of a stair, I stopped, eased back against the rough wall, raised my head, and shouted.

"Ryan! Jason! Wait!" But I knew it was too late. I heard the truck going down the highway. The stairwell above me seemed to magnify the sound. I was alone in this fortress — locked in for the night. Why had everyone left me?

True, nobody had seen me start up the tower stairs, but everyone knew I was in the museum. Surely they didn't think I had walked on home.

I sat down on one step and rested my feet on the step below. I would simply sit here until someone came to my rescue. But what if nobody came? If I dozed I might lose my balance and plunge over the side of the staircase. I opened my eyes wide, peering into the blackness.

As I sat there trying to decide what to do next, something crawled across my bare arm. Spider? Roach? Flinging the insect from me, I leaped to my feet. I couldn't wait here, not in this bug-infested darkness.

Pressing my back against the wall and with my arms outstretched against the masonry, I eased on down the twist of stairs. My fingers were stiff, cold rods scraping mortar loose from the wall. I heard it hit the metal steps and plunk down to the cement many feet below.

Something whizzed by my left ear, missing my flesh but brushing my hair. A bat! In my fright my foot slipped and I almost plunged off the unprotected side of the stairs. Now my sense of balance was gone, banished by height and darkness. To move was to risk injury or death.

"Sit down, Allison," I ordered myself. "Sit. Now scoot." Following my own commands, I scooted on my fanny from one step to the next, fearing every moment that the bat might return to tangle itself in my hair. But terror urged me downward.

After what seemed like hours, I reached the bottom of the stairs. Groping blindly, I felt for the light switch that I had turned on earlier. I found it, but now it wouldn't work. But of course not. Jason had pulled a master switch inside the front door when we had entered the museum. Surely he had pulled it again when he left.

I had no idea which direction I had come from, so once again I sat down to wait. Had someone purposely locked me in this fortress? The question whirled in my mind. Gilda's pranks had been frightening. The tapping on my ceiling had been harmless, but this stunt was different. This was no prank. I could have been killed had I fallen from the open spiral stairs. And even now I resisted moving for fear I would plunge into the citadel cistern. I had no idea where it was. I only knew that I had seen it earlier in the evening and that it was somewhere in the vicinity of the stairs to the tower.

Leaning against a dank wall, I tried to make myself comfortable. I closed my eyes, yet I fought off sleep. I counted to a hundred by ones, by twos, and by threes. I was beginning to count by fours when I heard a door open and saw a light flash on.

Although I wanted to call out, to shout for help, I crushed the desire. Cold sweat trickled down the backs of my legs. Who had returned to the fortress to find me? I held my breath, waiting.

"Allison! Allison, are you here?" Jason's voice wavered down the corridor. I leaped up. I wouldn't let Jason find me here alone. Frantically I sought a hiding place.

Chapter Twelve

"Allison! Where are you, Allison?"

This time Grams s voice pierced the silence. I felt my heart pound in relief.

"Gram! Gram! Here I am. Here by the tower steps." I dashed down a hallway in the direction of the light and of my grandmother's voice and all but fell into her outstretched arms.

"Allison! I'm so sorry." Gram patted my shoulder, tears welling in her eyes. "How horrible this must have been for you. Jason and I came back just as soon as we realized what had happened, didn't we, Jason?"

"That's right, Allison. We did." Jason tugged down on his shirt sleeves. "Bunny thought you were riding with Ryan and me. I had a few more chores to do after she and Vondetta and Gilda finished their tasks, so they drove on home. Ryan and I called to you, and when you didn't answer, we decided that you had gone on with Bunny. You're all right, aren't you?"

"Yes, I'm fine," I replied icily. "I'm sorry to be such a bother. I climbed to the top of the tower for the view, but I had no idea I'd be left alone in here."

Gram took my arm and we walked to Jason's car. Jason turned out the museum lights, locked the door, and said hardly a word on the ride home.

I was so unnerved by the time we reached Allamanda House that I gladly accepted Gram's invitation to spend the night downstairs on her pull-out bed. But long after we had said our good nights I lay wide awake.

I couldn't believe my ordeal in the tower had been an accident. Someone was starting to play rough. But who had seen me go to the tower? I wondered if someone had deliberately encouraged the others to leave the museum without me. I was well aware that a fall from the stairs or a plunge into the cistern could have killed me. Who wanted me out of the way? And why?

Again I mentally considered all the suspects. Perhaps Vondetta or Gilda had said, "Let's go on. Allison's coming with Jason." Then I thought carefully about Jason. He was the person who had the most reason to be angry at me over the decision not to sell Allamanda House. But surely it couldn't have been Jason. Jason and I were friends. I remembered Jason's kiss, remembered how he looked at me on our last date. We were more than friends.

Ryan? Earlier in the evening Ryan had brought me home in a huff, and later he hadn't even bothered to return to the museum to see if I was all right. I hated to suspect Ryan, but I did. Under his carefree exterior Ryan had a hard streak that chilled me. But I couldn't figure out why he would want to hurt me. Surely he wasn't jealous of my artistic ability. I almost laughed at that thought.

But this was no time for laughter. I wondered how badly Ryan had wanted to own Allamanda House. He had mentioned buying it from Jason at a later date. But now that Jason would not be the owner, maybe Ryan saw his own hope of owning Allamanda House banished from existence. And I was the cause. I sighed and considered the advantage of being an amoeba.

I lay awake until pale shadows of dawn began to creep across the walls. At sunrise Gram closed the window shutters to encourage me to rest, but even in the semidarkness sleep was a will-o'-the-wisp. I rose and ate breakfast with Gram. As soon as the stores were open, I drove to town, purchased a new lock for my door, and returned to Allamanda House to try to install it.

"Better let me help," Ryan said.

My pounding had masked the sound of his footsteps in the hallway, and I jumped in surprise.

"I managed to screw a bolt to the inside of this door a while back," I said. "But I'm getting nowhere with this lock."

"The wood in these old houses is resinous heart pine," Ryan said. "It hardens with age. That's why the Bahama houses have withstood everything from hurricanes to termites." Taking the hammer from me, Ryan studied the new lock and its fittings before he began removing the old lock.

"Why aren't you out fishing?" I blurted, uneasy in Ryan's presence.

"I have an appointment at the courthouse this morning," Ryan said. "The crew can manage without me now and then."

I wondered about Ryan's words. The courthouse was open until five o'clock and the *Blue Dolphin* docked at four. Yet Ryan had no reason to lie to me. And if he had tried to harm me last night, why was he being so helpful now? My mind whirled with unanswered questions.

When Ryan finished installing the lock, I thanked him politely. Then I hurried into my room and bolted myself in. Pressing my ear to the door, I listened to hear if Ryan's footsteps stopped at his room or if they went on down the stairs, but I couldn't tell.

Somehow my room seemed more like a wooden prison than like a refuge. Was Ryan waiting nearby, listening for my footsteps? And what about Jason?

This was madness. If I were to stay here with Gram until Sunday I had to believe that last night's experience had been the result of an accident, a misunderstanding.

I needed to talk to Jason, but apparently he had left Allamanda House early. I wished I could think of some small peace offering to give to Jason along with my apology. But Jason was so austere in his habits that I had no idea of what sort of thing would please him.

Suddenly I remembered the diary I had taken to the museum after my first hours of working in the storerooms. Jason had mentioned misplacing his grandmother's diary, and I had planned to check to see if that one was his. But in the confusion of clearing out the rooms, the matter had slipped my mind. Now was the time. Much as I hated returning to the museum, I grabbed my purse, my new door key, and my car keys. I left Allamanda House and drove to the museum.

Once inside the old fortress I inhaled the musty odor of ancient bricks and tried to forget last night's experience. I hurried to the main desk where a curator sat blinking his owlish eyes.

"I'm Allison Blue, Bunny Blue's granddaughter," I said.

"Yes, Miss Blue," the man replied. "May I help you today?"

"I hope so, sir. A few days ago I brought a box of items here from Allamanda House. Among them was a diary that I now have reason to believe belongs to one of my grandmother's tenants. Is there a chance that I might have the diary back?"

"That's an unusual request." The curator cleared his throat and hesitated for a moment. "But under the circumstances . . ." His voice trailed off. "I'll see if anyone has catalogued that box of items."

The curator disappeared into a small room behind his desk, and to my relief he soon returned carrying the leather-bound diary in his clawlike hand.

"Is this the book you had in mind?"

I opened the volume, glanced at the name, and nodded. "This is it. May I please take it back to Allamanda House? I know this is a strange request, but we never realized at the time that the diary didn't really belong to us. It was not ours to give."

"Take it," the man said. "In the event that the true owner cares to let us exhibit the book, we would be happy to do so."

I hurried from the museum before the curator could change his mind. As I opened my car door, I saw a slight movement in the ferns at the side of the old fort. Was I mistaken? Had I caught a glimpse of Ryan's blue skipper's cap? My scalp tightened. I wished I had been mistaken, but I knew I had not been. Ryan had followed me here, and obviously he wanted to keep his presence a secret.

Although it was broad daylight, I locked my car doors after I slipped beneath the wheel. I was shaking. Surely no one could harm me here on this balmy morning on a main street of Key West. I was just allowing last night's misunderstanding to shake me up.

I drove home by a roundabout route, checking in my rearview mirror to see if I were being followed. It would be easy to spot Ryan's truck on these narrow streets. But I saw nothing to indicate that Ryan was following me. I drove by the high school feeling like a foolish girl checking on her boy friend. But of course I saw nothing of Jason. It was too early for his lunch break.

Once back at Allamanda House I started to sprint upstairs to my room, but Gram called to me from the garden.

"Allison, can you spare a few minutes?"

"Certainly, Gram. What do you have in mind?"

"I'd like to prune this vanilla vine, and I need someone to hold the poinsettia branches back so that I won't accidentally snip them, too."

"Let me take my things to the house," I called. "Then I'll be right with you."

Deciding not to keep Gram waiting by dashing upstairs, I hurried to the living room and laid the diary and my purse on a chair by the desk.

As usual the garden was shaded at this time of the morning, and when I joined Gram I found her enjoying its coolness. Gram had been watering her plants, and a green hose stretched across the red brick path. I inhaled the scent of the damp earth as I lifted the scarlet poinsettia leaves from the path of Gram's shears.

"That orange tree is so heavy with fruit that I may have to prop up the limbs to keep them from breaking," Gram said when she finished her pruning.

"That sounds like a two-person job. What shall we use for a prop?"

Gram went to the far corner of a potting shed that was nothing more than a tin roof supported by four square posts. Returning with a notched pole, she placed its groove under an orange-laden limb and pushed. I helped, and soon the branch rested neatly on the pole.

"Gram! I'd like to paint this tree." I backed up to get a better perspective. "It's unique."

"Watch out for the cistern!" Gram called. "It's right behind you."

I sidestepped quickly enough to avoid stumbling on the low cistern wall.

"Why don't you get your easel and paint right now?" Gram asked. "There's nothing special to be done today."

"I have some letters to write," I said, hedging. I wanted to study the diary I had brought home before I showed it to Jason. If the diary weren't really his, it might only disappoint him and put me in a worse position with him than before. "Anyway, Gram, I'd like to try to paint this orange tree by moonlight. I get some interesting effects with pallid lighting."

Gram shrugged. "As you wish. I'm sure the tree will be here day and night."

I went to the living room, picked up my purse and the diary, and hurried to my room. After locking myself inside, I sat down with the diary and began to read. The entries were prosaic, and I soon tired of trying to decipher the spidery handwriting. Carrying the book downstairs, I showed it to Gram.

"I retrieved it from the museum because I thought it might be Jason's. The first part of it was written by a Sarah Murdock. Then, later on, the handwriting changes. I haven't discovered who wrote that part of it. Murdock — that name seems familiar."

"Murdock," Gram said thoughtfully. Then she shook her head. "The name means nothing to me. But it could belong to Jason. I had a lady come to help me clean a few months ago. She could have carried the diary to the storeroom. If you're through looking at it, lay it on my desk. I'll take a peek at it sometime this afternoon."

"I know where I've seen that name," I said, remembering. "At the cemetery! I saw a vase that we discarded from the storeroom on a grave, and the name on the grave marker was Murdock. What do you make of that?"

"Must be the trash man's family," Gram said. "He must have picked up the vase and found a use for it. By the way, have you seen Jason yet?"

"No, Gram. I'm almost sure he's avoiding me. I was stupid to get myself locked in the museum last night. Drat it, Gram. Why didn't I have sense enough to make sure I got to speak to Jason privately before I made that announcement!"

"We were all keyed up," Gram said. "Don't blame yourself so. You called the school. You left a message. That's all you could do. I just hope I haven't put you in bad with Jason by asking you to speak in my behalf. Jason's a good, steady man, Allison. You could do a lot worse."

"I'm far from ready to settle down, Gram. You're rushing me."

"Settle down" — I doubted that I would ever be ready to settle down. First I had thought I was in love with Ron Baker. Then Jason had fascinated me, and later, Ryan. The only thing I knew for sure was that the thought of Ron no longer made my heart beat faster. My thoughts swayed between Jason and Ryan. And how foolish! Jason was angry with me, and I was half afraid of Ryan.

That afternoon I played tourist and

146

visited both the Hemingway House and the Audubon House. By evening I was ready to rest. I saw nothing of Jason, so I had no chance to either return the diary or apologize. Gram and I shared a light supper, then we settled down to read the evening paper. As the moon rose, I remembered my desire to paint the orange tree by moonlight. But the thought of venturing into the garden alone chilled me. After last night's misadventure I was wary.

"Gram, would you sit in the garden with me while I paint?"

Gram hesitated only a moment. "Why, certainly, Allison. You're frightened, aren't you? I'm so sorry. I do want your vacation here to be pleasant. After last night I can understand how you feel, but accidents do happen."

"I'm not really frightened," I said. "Let's just say that I'm going to be more careful from now on. If you'll sit with me in the garden, I'll carry a chair for you."

It took me two trips to lug easel and paints and our two chairs to the garden, but I thought the effort worthwhile. By sitting near the cistern, I could get a full view of the orange tree complete with dangling fruit and propped limb.

"You're good for me, Allison," Gram

said. "I hardly remember the last time I sat in the garden by moonlight. I'd forgotten how lovely it is. The yellow jessamine is beginning to bloom. Smell the fragrance?"

Inhaling the scent of the jessamine, I painted, trying to capture on canvas the ethereal quality of the moonlight slanting onto the orange tree. Gram rocked, and the slight squeaking of her chair was the only sound except that of the wind whispering in the palms.

If someone had stood up in church and banged on a pie tin the sound couldn't have been more incongruous than the sudden jangling of the telephone inside Allamanda House. I flinched at its loudness and suddenness.

"Who could be calling me at this time of the night?" Gram jumped up and headed for the house. "I'll be right back, Allison."

I listened to the measured jangling of the telephone. When the sound broke off in the middle of a ring, I knew Gram had picked up the receiver. Leaning over my easel, I prepared more paint, adding, mixing, and adding, until I achieved the shade I was seeking. I was leaning to the right to get a better perspective when I began to fall.

At first I thought a chair leg had slipped

into a hole in the ground. But then I felt sure someone had shoved me. For a fleeting moment I flailed my arms in an effort to regain my balance, but my chair toppled and crashed. My shoulder grazed the cistern wall. Then I plunged into a dizzying blackness.

Chapter Thirteen

For a few moments after I regained consciousness I had no idea of where I was. My left arm felt numb, and shooting pains stabbed through my shoulder. Where was I? What had happened?

As I tried to sit up, I felt an oozing dampness beneath me. Then something nudged at my leg. Groping in the blackness, I touched a bulky, ridged plate that moved under the weight of my hand. A turtle! Even in the darkness I knew I had touched a turtle, and I recoiled in horror. In that moment I guessed where I was. A scream seared my throat.

It seemed that I screamed for hours before a beam of light wavered above my head.

"Allison! Allison!" Fear quavered in Gram's voice. "Don't be afraid. We'll get you out of there. Allison? Can you hear me, Allison?"

"Yes, Gram." I stopped screaming. Revulsion at the thought of sharing space with a turtle forced me to my feet, although a lightning pain struck my shoulder once again. The agony was so intense I couldn't even look up to see what was going on above me.

"I'm lowering a chair to you." Ryan's voice sent hope surging through me. "There are ropes attached to the chair, Allison. Are you able to sit on it?"

I waited until the chair thumped onto the bottom of the cistern. "Yes," I called feebly. "I can sit on the chair."

"Good," Ryan called. "Can you use your hands? I've laced a belt through the spindles on the chair back. If you can use your hands, strap yourself into the chair with the belt. Can you do that?"

"I th-think so." I eased onto the chair. My left hand hurt less than the right one, and somehow I managed to buckle the belt around my waist.

"Tell us when you're ready." Ryan's voice echoed hollowly against the concrete wall of the cistern. "Don't hurry, Allison. Be thorough."

"I'm r-ready," I called at last.

"Hang on," Ryan ordered. "We'll try to be gentle, but this may jar you."

My fingers ached from clutching the chair so tightly. I felt myself rising inch by inch — up, up. The journey to the top of

the cistern seemed to take hours. Sometimes I felt the chair slip back down. But at
last my head peeked above the cistern rim
and I saw Gram staring at me, her face
etched with horror. When at last the chair
was out of the cistern and I was un-
strapped from it, Ryan steadied me on my
feet and Gilda appeared at my side. Gilda
had used her great strength to help Ryan
hoist the chair.

"I've called Dr. Beardsley," Gram said.
"Are you badly hurt?"

"I can't tell," I said. "My shoulder . . ."

"How did it happen?" Ryan demanded.
"Did you fall?"

"Yes." I tried to sound positive. If I admitted that I thought I had been pushed, it
would put me on the defensive. "I leaned
too far to the right trying to get a better
perspective on the orange tree. I forgot
about the cistern."

Before I had to explain further, Dr.
Beardsley arrived. He lived up to his name
by wearing a beard that made him look like
one of the men pictured on a certain
cough-drop box, but I was glad to see him.
He and Gram helped me to my room.

Dr. Beardsley checked me over gently
but firmly, treated my scrapes and cuts,
and then placed my right arm in a sling.

"You've dislocated a collarbone, Miss Blue. A few days' rest with the arm in a sling should make you mend. You're a lucky girl. You could have been killed in a fall like that."

I was so fascinated with the way Dr. Beardsley's beard bobbed up and down when he talked that I momentarily forgot about my accident. Then, remembering my manners, I said, "Thank you for coming out at night, Doctor. I really appreciate it."

After the doctor left, Gram, Gilda, and Ryan stepped into my room.

"I'm going to hire workmen to cap that cistern first thing tomorrow," Gram said. "I blame myself for that accident, Allison."

"Don't blame yourself, Gram." I tried to smile, although one side of my face felt sore and swollen. "This accident was my own silly fault. And Ryan and Gilda, how can I ever thank you for rescuing me!"

"It was just turn about," Gilda said, her voice booming. "Turn about for what you did for me."

Ryan said nothing, but his eyes bored into my face until I looked away in confusion. I was glad when everyone left me alone for the night. As soon as I was sure my rescuers were out of earshot, I forced myself from bed and locked my door.

Ryan knew. Ryan knew I had lied about falling. I could tell by the way he had looked at me. Yet how could he be so sure? I was only ninety-nine per cent sure myself. I thought I had felt hands shoving my chair, but there was a one per cent chance that I had been wrong.

Who would want to push me into the cistern? Perhaps the same person who saw to it that I was abandoned in the museum. Perhaps Ryan was the guilty one. He certainly was on the scene quickly enough after it had happened. Maybe his big rescue act was a cover for a dastardly deed.

The doctor had given me a sleeping pill. Much as I wanted to stay awake and think about my plight, I felt myself grow drowsy, felt reality slipping away.

The next morning I felt brittle as glass. Surely if I moved I would crack and shatter to bits. Gram offered to carry breakfast to me, but I insisted on going downstairs to eat. Dr. Beardsley had ordered me to move around. And the doctor was right.

I moved slowly, but the more I forced myself to bend, the easier bending became. While I was sitting at the kitchen table, Vondetta paid Gram a visit, leaving a check for her room rent. When she left, Gram waved the check gleefully at me.

"See what you've done for me, Allison! Your plan is working beautifully."

It worked beautifully if one overlooked being shoved into a cistern as a direct result, I thought. But I smiled at Gram. Maybe I was wrong. Maybe my fall had been an accident. I would try to believe that I had fallen, but at the same time I would be on guard. I would see to it that there would be no more accidents.

In a few short days I would be leaving Allamanda House. And I was glad. It hurt me to remember how eagerly I had come here, wanting to know my grandmother more intimately. But my troubles were certainly not Gram's fault. I would enjoy her company no matter how I felt about her tenants.

Now a whole day stretched ahead like an endless expanse of time. I rested for a while after breakfast. Then I forced myself to exercise by strolling through the garden. But even by daylight I still thought the garden eerie, and I soon wandered back into the house.

In the afternoon I napped. When I awakened, I decided to read a bit more of the diary I had retrieved from the museum. I walked downstairs and looked for the book on Gram's desk. I would read a bit, then return the diary to Jason when he came in from school.

"Lost something?" Gram asked, entering the room.

"The diary," I said. "I thought I'd read a bit in it before I returned it to Jason. Surely I'll see him sometime today. The diary was right here on your desk, wasn't it?"

"Of course," Gram said. "Look under that newspaper."

After searching the desk top thoroughly, I knew the diary was gone. "Now who could have taken it?" I asked Gram. "I thought it quite dull."

"I hardly had a chance to look at it," Gram said. "Perhaps it'll turn up somewhere. It couldn't walk off, you know."

"It didn't walk off," Jason said, strolling into the living room from the porch. "Pardon me for eavesdropping, but I heard your discussion from outside. I was just coming in to tell you that I saw my diary on your desk at noon and I took the liberty of borrowing it."

"Oh, Jason!" I exclaimed. "I'm so glad it is your diary. I've felt really guilty about Gram's withdrawing Allamanda House from the market. I checked up on the diary as sort of a peace offering. I accidentally took it to the museum, but the curator was nice enough to let me have it back."

"I hope you didn't have to do battle for it," Jason said, eyeing my sling and bruises.

"You haven't heard?" Gram asked. "Allison took a tumble down the cistern last night. Luckily she wasn't too badly hurt, but she gave us a terrible scare."

"I'm sorry to hear that," Jason said. "If there's anything I can do . . ."

"I'm on the mend now," I assured him. "I don't feel up to much physical activity, so I thought I'd read in that diary for a while."

"I'd like to oblige you," Jason said, "but I've planned to copy some family data from it this afternoon. Of course, I'll be glad to share it with you later. In fact I may return it to the museum eventually. It is a museum piece and it should be kept on display."

Jason left us as quickly as he had arrived, and I was only mildly disappointed at being denied the privilege to peruse the old diary. The important thing was that Jason didn't seem angry about my part in the plan to keep Allamanda House in the Blue family for a while longer.

Jason's good will meant more to me than

I had realized, and I was sorry I had forgotten to tell him the addresses of the other Bahamas' houses on the island that I had seen listed for sale.

I entertained myself the rest of the afternoon by reading a colorful booklet on the history of Key West. Before supper I took another brief stroll. Then I dozed in my room until a knock on my door awakened me.

"Just a minute," I called as I ran a comb through my hair and straightened my rumpled skirt. Then, after easing across the room and opening the door, I stood face to face with Ryan.

"I've come to ask you for a date tonight," Ryan said. "Are you free?"

"Oh, Ryan! I can't go out anywhere with all these scrapes and bruises. And this sling is so cumbersome. I just don't feel like going out."

"Who said anything about going out?" Ryan asked. "I've checked with Bunny, and she's loaned me her kitchen for an hour or so. We'll spend a quiet evening right here at Allamanda House. I'll fry snapper fingers if you and Bunny will be my guests. And incidentally, Bunny has already accepted."

I laughed in spite of myself. Maybe I had

been wrong about Ryan. He seemed sincere, and his friendly manner was hard to resist. If I had angered him on our last date, he seemed to have recovered. I had promised myself to be careful, but surely no harm could come to me right in Gram's kitchen.

"Okay, Ryan. It's a date."

Ryan surprised both Gram and me with his prowess in the kitchen. He fried the snapper to a golden brown, tossed the salad to perfection. And the Key lime pie — well, Ryan admitted he had purchased it from the delicatessen.

After we finished eating, I did my best to help Ryan with the dishes. Gram went to the living room, leaving us alone.

"I want to talk with you, Allison," Ryan said. "Let's go out on the porch."

I led the way, trying to walk firmly and surely.

"Allison, I don't want to frighten you, but I think you're in grave danger."

I sat down on the porch swing and Ryan joined me. "What sort of danger?" I felt my spine tingle as Ryan voiced the thought I had tried to keep at the back of my mind.

"I'm not sure," Ryan admitted. "But I think Jason could bear watching. It's just a feeling I have, Allison. I can prove nothing against Jason."

"Then I think you should say nothing," I snapped, surprised at my own show of temper. "Just because Jason's introverted and very much of a loner is no reason to suspect him of anything. Being unable to buy Allamanda House is a great disappointment to him, but I talked with him only this afternoon. I'm sure he bears no grudge against me for my part in Gram's decision not to sell her home."

"If that's the way you feel, then I'll say good night." Ryan stood, a red flush coloring his neck and face. "But I hope you'll remember what I've just said to you. I hope you'll remember it and heed it. Two accidents in two days! That's a bit much."

Ryan strode from the porch and through the garden. He sped away in his truck before I could say anything. But I hadn't wanted to say anything. I felt sure that Ryan had been following me when I went to the museum for the diary. He had appeared all too conveniently at the cistern last night. And now he was trying to set me against Jason.

Perhaps Ryan was jealous. I could think of no other reason why he should go to the trouble of warning me against Jason. Jason had attracted Vondetta away from Ryan. It was only natural that Ryan should be jealous. Jason was handsome and he was wealthy. It was easy to understand why Ryan envied him. I tried to forget Ryan's warning as I prepared for bed.

I was stiff and sore, but by Saturday I was feeling better. Saturday was a day for lazing about for everyone except Ryan, who took his fishing boat out as usual. Gilda went to the Laundromat, Vondetta slept late, and Jason drove away on some errand. Gram and I were home alone. Gram was in the garden when I heard the wind come up. The smell of the sea hung in the air as doors banged shut, window shutters rattled, and a dark cloud masked the sun.

I still felt stiff and sore, but I managed to go to each upstairs room and shut the windows against the rain that was just beginning to beat a loud tattoo on the tin roof.

As I passed through Jason's room, I saw his diary lying on his desk. I picked it up. Jason had said I could read it. And since he was out, it was obvious that he wasn't using it at the moment.

Carrying the diary through the gloom to my room, I snapped on my desk lamp and began reading where I had left off before. Now the diary entries seemed more interesting. There was a day-by-day account of a sea captain who moved his house from the Bahamas to Key West. Then there was a woman's lamenting account of her beautiful and gentle granddaughter marrying beneath her "station." I was amused at first, but the woman's dire prophecy about her grandson-in-law seemed to come true as she wrote that he turned to gambling, losing his fortune as well as his home. Clearly this was the same story Jason had told me about his parents.

I stopped reading as I heard a tapping on my ceiling. Surely someone wasn't trying to frighten me right in broad daylight. Closing the diary, I carried it back to Jason's room. This time he was in.

"I borrowed this, Jason," I said, returning the diary. "The wind came up, and I saw it lying on your desk when I came in to close your window. Hope you don't mind."

"Not at all," Jason said. "Did you read much?"

"I just skipped through parts of it, sort of hit and miss. The handwriting's hard to decipher. But I'd like to look at it again sometime before I leave here. I really would. The more Key West lore I can absorb, the more feeling I'll have for my painting of Key West scenes. That means a lot to me, Jason."

Jason took the diary, thanked me, and abruptly closed his door. I had been about to tell him about the strange tapping on my ceiling, but the closed door was as definite as a "no trespassing" sign. I walked back to my room. The tapping sounded again. Curiosity got the best of me. Someone was on the third floor, but who? Surely not Ryan. He was out on the *Blue Dolphin*. Jason was in his room, Gilda was out, and Gram was downstairs. Vondetta?

Slowly I mounted the steep steps and hoisted myself from one stair to the next. At the scant landing I found the door to the east room closed. When I opened it, Vondetta jumped in surprise.

I had guessed that I might find her here, but I had no idea what she was doing.

"What is your business up here, Vondetta?" I sniffed the cloying scent of heliotrope.

Vondetta rose from where she had been kneeling over a loose floor board, her face a hard mask of bravado. "I might ask you the same question, Allison. As far as I know, Bunny hasn't forbidden anyone to come to the third floor. The view from the widow's walk is terrific!"

"But you're not enjoying the view," I said. "Nor am I. I came up to see who was tapping on my ceiling. I thought someone was trying to frighten me — again. But clearly that's not what you have in mind. I can see now that you're searching for something. Care to tell me about it?"

Vondetta's face flushed, but she recaptured her poise quickly. "I'll make a deal with you, Allison. We'll be partners." Vondetta's eyes glittered.

"What sort of a deal and what sort of partners?" I asked, puzzled and wary.

"We'll split the treasure fifty-fifty when we find it," Vondetta said.

"What treasure, Vondetta? Are you kidding?"

"I've never been more serious." Now Vondetta batted her false eyelashes, her eyes wide. "Don't you know the history of this old house? It was built in the Bahamas and shipped here by an old sea captain."

"Gram told me that," I said. "That makes Allamanda House a treasure trove of some sort?"

"That's what I think." Vondetta leaned toward me, whispering. "Years ago pirates roamed the coves and inlets both here and in the Bahamas. Commodore David Porter commanded a fleet that routed the pirates from this area. But don't you think some of them might have left their treasure behind? And maybe a sea captain found it and hid it in his home. Why would anyone bother to tear a house down and ship it across the sea unless it contained something more valuable than just wood?"

"Vondetta, you have a wild imagination and you've learned just a smattering of history. I'm glad you've told me these things, but I'll never be your partner. Are you the one who persuaded the others to leave me in the museum? Did you push me into the cistern? Did you think that by getting rid of me you would have the whole treasure hunt to yourself?"

Vondetta spluttered. "How dare you! Don't you know me better than that? What sort of a person do you think I am!"

"In my book you're nothing but a gold digger," I said, feeling almost sure that at last I had found the person who had tried to harm me. Of course, I could prove nothing, but in my mind I knew. Vondetta had been after treasure and I was a threat to her progress. She could have fooled Gram, but I was another matter.

Now that I was thinking, I realized that Vondetta had probably heard me the night I had come up here to investigate the tapping. She had undoubtedly hidden up on the widow's walk. I had not thought to look for an intruder up on the roof. Vondetta's face flushed an angry red that rose from her neck to her hairline as I continued.

"I'm on to you, Vondetta. When you thought Ryan was going to buy Allamanda House, you were his girl, his bride-to-be. Then, when it looked as if Jason would be the new owner, you dropped Ryan and made an obvious play for Jason. So now that you know Gram is keeping the house, you're offering me a partnership in your treasure-hunting scheme to keep me quiet. I want none of it, Vondetta. None."

To my surprise, tears welled in Vondetta's eyes, and a rivulet of mascara ran down her left cheek. She looked like a pathetic child playing grown-up in her mother's cosmetics.

"I shouldn't have expected you to understand." Vondetta choked back sobs. "You're Miss Somebody and your kind never understands how the Miss Nobodys of the world feel. You've got talent. You're an artist. You have a good job. You can go places and do things. But I'm just a nothing. My parents were divorced when I was fifteen, and I've been on my own since then. I've no special talent or I wouldn't be waiting tables in that hash house. Don't you understand that who I marry may be the most important factor in my life?"

"Marriage is an important thing to consider in anyone's life," I countered.

"But my choice of husband will tell the world who I am. If I ever have any status, it will come through my choice of husband. You shouldn't blame me for trying to pick the best man I can find. And I can't help it if sometimes the best means the richest. That's the way the world is. I can't buck it."

I felt my attitude toward Vondetta softening. The museum? The cistern? In the eyes of the law a person is innocent until proven guilty, and I could prove nothing against Vondetta. My experiences at the museum and the cistern could both have been accidents. When Gram took someone under her wing, there was usually a good reason for her choice. Vondetta needed a friend — an understanding heart, and I was the only one around.

"Vondetta, every girl should put her best foot forward, but not at the expense of others. If you dislike who you are, then be someone different."

I paused for a moment. Then I continued before Vondetta could interrupt. I didn't care if she thought I was preaching. This was no popularity contest.

"Vondetta, what you make of your life is strictly up to you. And you're young. You'll have better luck if you search for treasure in a school building."

"What sort of treasure would be there?" Vondetta scowled.

"A treasure of the mind," I said. "Think it over. And think carefully. An education could change your whole life. It's within your grasp if you really want it. Anyone can work their way through college these days. I'll say nothing of any of this to Gram, and you needn't tell her unless you want to. I wouldn't blame her for smiling if she knew that you honestly thought there was a treasure hidden in this old house."

I went back downstairs, still wondering about Vondetta. I stretched out on my bed, and no more tapping disturbed me as I napped.

Chapter Fourteen

By Sunday my scrapes and cuts were healing well and I discarded my sling. I was stronger, and I was glad of that for I had to begin packing. I planned to drive to Miami before dawn the next morning and report for work by nine o'clock. As I packed I kept my door locked, but I was no longer constantly on guard against some unknown enemy.

Vondetta had denied trying to harm me, and I believed in my heart that she was telling the truth. The incident in the museum and the fall in the cistern had been accidents. I felt no threat from Vondetta. She had said nothing more to me, and there had been no more tapping on my ceiling.

I thought back over my two weeks at Allamanda House. I had dated Jason. Although he fascinated me, he was an enigma — somber, silent — revealing little of his inner nature. Sometimes I had found myself caring for him so deeply that I wondered if I were falling in love with him. Or did I merely feel sorry for him? We had hardly spent any time together without Jason reminding me of the terrible beating his father had given him, of his scars and facial injuries.

Although Ryan had seldom asked me out, he still fascinated me. I was a bit frightened of Ryan. He made me uneasy. What was it about him? I had no answer. But I had limited my conversations with Ryan to discussions of art or brief showings of my current work-in-progress, for I had tried to cram all the painting I could into these last few days before I had to leave for Miami.

This morning Gram had gone to church. After I finished my packing, I decided to read. When I found no books in my room that interested me, I rapped on Jason's door.

"Jason?" I smiled when he appeared in his doorway. "If you're not using your family diary, would you let me borrow it for a few minutes until Gram gets home from church?"

"Sorry, Allison." Jason shook his head. "I've returned the diary to the museum. That's where it really belongs. I copied down a few items from it and returned it a few days ago. I didn't realize that you were still interested in it. Excuse me, please, but

I have to dress for an important appointment."

Jason closed his door and left me standing there. I sighed, wondering why Jason had returned the diary. He had known I wanted to see it again. Surely I had made that clear. And he knew I was leaving tomorrow. Perhaps he was subtly trying to get even with me for helping Gram keep Allamanda House. Would I never understand this man? I was still standing in front of Jason's closed door when Ryan dashed up the stairs.

"Allison!" He smiled as if he were pleased to see me. "I was just coming to knock on your door." Ryan held up three tickets. "I have seats for *The Lion In Winter* at the Waterfront Playhouse. Since it's the last performance and also your last night in Key West, I'm hoping you and Bunny will go with me. I'd like to take you both out once more before you go to Miami."

How could I refuse? I knew I would enjoy the play, and it wouldn't be fair to turn Ryan down and keep Gram from having an evening out.

"Yes, Ryan. I'd enjoy attending the play with you. I'll have to check with Gram, but as far as I know she has nothing special planned for us this evening."

"Great!" Ryan beamed. "I'll call for you around seven-thirty. Curtain time's eight o'clock."

Ryan dashed back down the steps, leaving me still standing before Jason's door. Suddenly I was elated that I had accepted Ryan's invitation. It would be fun to go out with a man who smiled now and then. It would be fun even if it was a farewell party.

When Gram came home from church, I told her of Ryan's invitation. She was delighted. She had wanted to have a big going-away dinner for me, but I had objected. I wanted the two of us to have time alone to visit.

Our meal was pleasant, and by the time the dishes were cleared away I had made Gram promise to visit me in Miami just as soon as I found a place to live and was settled. Since we had a late evening planned, Gram excused herself to go to her room to nap. But I refused to spend my last afternoon in Key West sleeping.

I got into my car, intending to tour the island one last time. As I drove along, my thoughts returned to Jason. The more I considered him, the more my irritation grew. Jason had known that I wanted to see that diary again. He had deliberately returned it to the museum without giving me the opportunity. Was there something in it that he wanted to hide? That was almost a ridiculous thought. If he had wanted to hide something he would have been more careful with the diary. But I had nothing else to do until Gram awakened from her nap. I decided to check on my hunch. The museum was open and I decided to relieve my curiosity.

Driving the short distance to the museum, I parked my car at the doorway and hurried inside.

"I beg your pardon," I said to the curator. "But would it be possible for me to see the Murdock diary once more?"

He glanced up at me, his owllike eyes magnified by his thick glasses. "I'm sorry, Miss Blue. That diary is really rather fragile. I can't allow it to go in and out of here as if this were a circulating library. Jason Wymington has returned it to me and here it's going to remain."

"Jason Wymington?" I asked, puzzled.

"Excuse me. Jason McKillum. You young folks! I've known Jason Wymington since he was a baby and his folks lived on Stock Island. Then he up and changes his name and expects everyone to remember."

"I didn't know Jason had changed his name," I said. "My grandmother never mentioned it to me."

"She probably didn't know," he said. "The family moved around a lot. But I thought you'd read the family diary. McKillum was Jason's mother's maiden name. And the name on the title page, Murdock, refers to Jason's great-grandmother on his mother's side."

Now I understood. Jason was so consumed with hatred for his father that he had even forsaken his name. But I had not guessed that from reading the diary. Few last names were mentioned. The writers of the diary had used first names, evidentally assuming that the entries were of concern only to them.

Murdock — that had been the name I had noticed in the cemetery. Jason was the one who had taken the discarded vase. He thought enough of his mother to care for the family grave. I admired and respected him for that. But I still wanted to see the diary once more.

"Could I look at the diary while I'm here in the museum?" I asked.

The curator glared at me over the top of his glasses. "I suppose there'd be no harm in that if you're going to insist."

Shoving his chair back from his desk, he pulled out a drawer, picked up a key ring in his clawlike fingers, and hobbled to a glass display case. Unlocking its door, he brought out the diary and handed it to me.

"There's a chair right by my desk," he said. "You may sit there while you read."

I felt like a school child on probation, but I did as the old man said. Soon the diary held my complete attention, and I was oblivious to the trickle of tourists who paid their dollar admissions and drifted in and out of the museum.

I had been reading for a long time when suddenly I paused. I had come to a reference to a home called Allamanda House. What a coincidence! Pulling a notebook and pen from my purse, I had just started to copy that particular passage from the diary when a shadow fell across my paper. I looked up into Jason's face.

"I thought I might find you here." Jason's eyes were opaque as agates, revealing nothing. "Bunny asked me to give you a message. She and Gilda are driving to visit a friend. She said she would be back before seven. She wanted you to go, but she couldn't find you."

My attitude toward Jason softened as I realized that he had gone out of his way to be helpful.

"Thank you, Jason. But you needn't have

driven all the way over here. Gram could have left a note for me. But, Jason! Guess what I just found in this diary? Someone in your family has written about another grand old home called Allamanda House."

No sooner had I uttered the words than I wished I could yank them back. I couldn't read the expression that crossed Jason's face. Excitement? Rage? Hatred? How could I have been so stupid!

"Allamanda House." I met Jason's peculiar gaze and my voice faded to a whisper. "It's the same Allamanda House that Gram owns, isn't it? She said it was already named when she bought it. Allamanda House was your mother's family home. Allamanda House was the home your father gambled away. Oh, Jason! I'm so sorry. I thought you just wanted to restore a Bahamas' house, any Bahamas' house. I didn't know Allamanda House was so special to you."

"I realize you didn't know," Jason said, his face an unreadable mask. "I didn't expect you to know, and I don't want you to feel badly about it. I can understand your loyalty to your grandmother. You came here at her request, and I certainly don't blame you for anything you've done to help her retain the house."

"Thank you, Jason. That makes me feel a little better. Gram doesn't even know, does she? About Allamanda House, I mean?"

Jason shook his head. "After my father lost the house, it changed hands three or four times before your grandmother bought it. She was young, and she purchased it on the advice of a lawyer. He bought Allamanda House for her at a tax sale. My parents had moved from Key West long before your grandmother bought the house. I didn't want you to know all this, Allison."

"But I'm glad I found out," I said.

Jason shook his head. "I have a knack for saying the wrong thing. After I told you the diary was here, I knew I'd done nothing but arouse your curiosity. I knew you'd come here, and I figured that this time you'd stumble onto the truth."

"Jason, let's go tell Gram the whole story. Maybe once she understands the situation the two of you can work out something."

"We can't tell her now," Jason said. "I told you. She and Gilda have gone out. There was a note on her door. They won't be back until seven."

I sighed. So Gram hadn't really sent

Jason here. She may have talked to him, but he had merely read the note and taken it upon himself to come here. My mind was in a muddle. But now that I understood the why of things, I might be able to help in some way. I sighed again.

"Cheer up." Jason leaned down and kissed me on the forehead. "There's nothing that can be done about all this right now. But I have an idea that will take your mind off Allamanda House for a while. Turn that diary in and come with me."

I obeyed without question. Jason had kissed me. He had even smiled a little. We understood each other.

"Drive back to Allamanda House," Jason said. "I'll follow in my car. Get your easel and paints, and we'll go to the shrimp docks. This is your last chance. You still want to paint a shrimp boat, don't you?"

"Oh, yes," I said. "I was afraid I was going to have to leave before I had the opportunity to paint one, though. But, Jason, I don't want to be in anyone's way."

"Then let's go," Jason said. "The shrimp dock is a busy place, and the shrimping crews are made up of rough, tough fellows. But there's one boat in dry dock, and I'm supposed to be making repairs on it. I'll be right there in sight so you can paint without worrying about anything."

"The light will fade before long." I glanced at the sky.

"Maybe you could just make a pencil sketch — something to base a painting on later when you're in Miami."

I got into my car and drove home. Now I almost wished I hadn't told Ryan I would go to the play with him that night. But I wouldn't go back on my word. Surely Jason and I would be home in time for me to keep my date with Ryan and Gram. I couldn't sketch in the dark, and the sun would set around six o'clock.

Jason waited in his car while I hurried to my room, pulled my painting smock from my suitcase, and slipped it on.

Then, getting my easel and charcoal pencils from the storage closet, I carried them to Jason's car. He placed them on the back seat for me, and I slipped onto the front cushion beside him.

We drove to Key West Bight, stopping at an area known as Land's End Village. Jason parked his car as close to the shrimp docks as he could and we walked the rest of the way.

"Want to look aboard a shrimper before you begin to sketch?" Jason asked.

"Would it be all right? I mean we wouldn't be trespassing or anything?"

"It's all right," Jason said. "I have a permit to be aboard the *Stella Lou.* Lean your easel here against this palm tree for the time being. It'll be okay. We'll pick it up later."

Throngs of people milled through the area, but nobody was at the dry dock where the *Stella Lou* was moored. I stashed my easel in a safe place and followed Jason. A few of the white shrimp boats with their black nets and rigging bobbed gently in the bay. Old tires were lashed to the boat sides to keep the vessels from hitting each other in their narrow mooring berths.

"Where is everyone?" I asked.

"The shrimpers that are in are waiting for repairs," Jason said. "And I guess no boats are due to dock today. The shrimping crews stay out from one to three weeks at a time, depending on how long it takes them to net their cargo of pink gold."

"Pink gold!" I exclaimed. "What a picturesque name for shrimp."

"But an appropriate name." Jason tugged his shirt sleeves down over his scarred wrists. "The discovery that night trawling for shrimp yielded huge catches was as important to Key West as the discovery of gold was to California. Today the annual revenue from this gold exceeds ten million dollars."

"You're a natural schoolteacher," I said with a laugh. "I'll bet the kids fight to take your classes."

"Come on aboard." Jason helped me up a narrow gangplank and onto the *Stella Lou*, which was entirely out of the water. For a moment I was almost overcome by the fishy odor. A gull soared and wheeled overhead, but the only sound was the lapping of water against the sea wall.

Jason showed me inside the small cabin in the center of the boat. Then we left it and walked around the deck, stepping over nets, ropes, and chains. At one place Jason stooped and lifted a square floor hatch, revealing the darkness of the below-deck space.

"What's down there?" I asked.

"The engines," Jason said. "That's where I work. It's dark and smelly, but the pay's good. Want to take a peek?" Pulling a flashlight from his pocket, Jason pointed the beam down a narrow companionway leading into the hold — more like a ladder than a stairway.

"Only a peek," I said. "How can you stand to work in such an awful place?"

Jason didn't reply, and I took the flashlight from him and leaned forward to see if I could see an engine. When I first felt Jason's hand on my shoulder, I thought he was trying to steady me. But in the next moment I knew the truth. With a grunt that was almost a savage growl Jason shoved me toward the yawning hole.

Dropping the flashlight, I clutched wildly for support. My fingers snatched at Jason's shirt, caught for a moment, but it tore away. I fell into the stinking hold of the shrimp boat.

Too stunned to scream or even to move, I lay in a heap. I was trapped. I felt my heart stop beating as I heard Jason climbing down the ladder into this hot, smelly space. Slowly I turned to look at him, but his features were so twisted with hatred and rage that I hid my face in my arms, fully expecting to die in the next moment.

Chapter Fifteen

Holding my breath, I waited for the blows that never came. At last I had to gasp for air. I looked up and saw that Jason had hung the flashlight from a ceiling wire and that he was approaching me with a length of rope. Why struggle? I was still dazed from my fall. Jason could easily overpower me.

"What are you going to do?" I managed to stand up and back away from Jason.

"What do you think I'm going to do?" Jason sneered. "I'm going to tie you up so you'll never leave this boat."

"But why?" I kept inching backward. "Why? What good is leaving me tied here going to do you?"

"It's going to get me Allamanda House." Jason's voice rang with triumph. "Bunny Blue is a cream puff, a marshmallow. She's a spineless jellyfish. Without you as her ramrod, she'll fold up. Grief over your death will only hasten her collapse."

"My death! You can't get away with this, Jason!" A thud punctuated my words as I

183

bumped into the side of the boat and could retreat no farther.

Jason laughed, hysteria curling the edges of the sound. "Of course I can get away with it. The *Stella Lou* will be docked here for over two weeks. An engine part is on order, and I know it'll take at least that long for it to arrive. The boat's out of operation. Nobody will have reason to come aboard. And in two weeks' time you'll be quite dead. In fact you'll be dead long before that because I'm coming back here with a gun later tonight, when everyone's off the streets and the docks."

"It'll never work out for you," I warned. "Never. I'll scream. I'll —"

Jason flung me down onto my stomach. He bound my hands behind my back. I kicked and screamed, but Jason only laughed and ducked whenever my feet threatened him.

"Calm down." Jason yanked me to a sitting position. "I thought of this fate for your grandmother, but then I realized that I would be foolish to kill her. Someone else would inherit the house. I knew I had to get it legally. I had to buy Allamanda House."

I tilted my chin and kicked at Jason's shin, this time landing a painful blow.

For a moment Jason recoiled. Then he sprang at me with greater fury than before. "I've been kicked and beaten for the last time." With a heavy hand Jason knocked me flat. Then, jerking off my shoes, he grabbed my feet and began tying them together.

"You'll never get away with this." I gasped for air, but I was helpless.

Once he had subdued me, Jason smiled bitterly, his face darkly shadowed in the dim glow from the overhead flashlight.

"I'm sorry to have to do this to you, Allison. I really am."

"I suppose you were sorry when you locked me in the musuem and when you shoved me into the cistern," I said, suddenly knowing the truth.

"Yes, I really hated to do those things to you. We had some good times together, Allison. I wish our lives could have worked out differently."

I forced back tears, refusing to give Jason the satisfaction of seeing me cry in my fear and rage.

"If you were really sorry, you'd let me loose," I said.

"Right," Jason agreed. "I'm not all that sorry. Once you're out of my way, I'll persuade your grandmother to sell Allamanda

House to me. And on that day I will have gotten even with my father. I will have proved myself the better man."

"How do you figure that?" I decided to try to keep talking, to stall for time and hope for some miracle that would save me.

"My father was nothing but a bully, a child beater, and a drunken gambler. He wasn't even smart enough to hang on to the home that had been in my mother's family for generations. But I'll show the world that his son is made of better stuff. I'm going to turn Allamanda House into the showplace of the Keys. It will be written up in national magazines when I get through with it. People will drive for miles to see it. And the story of my life will be engraved on a bronze plaque that will hang on the lower porch. The plaque will tell the world what my father was and what I am."

Before I could say another word, Jason jerked my scarf from around my head and gagged me with it. Then, yanking the flashlight from the overhead wire, he climbed from the hold, replaced the floor hatch, and bolted it down.

I waited for my eyes to adjust to the darkness, but I could see nothing. Unrelieved blackness swallowed me. With a great effort I leaned back and tried to bang my feet against the side of the boat. Without shoes I could only make a dull thud. What would become of me? I knew all too well.

Jason was coming back. How long did I have to live before he returned to murder me? And Jason was going to get away with his scheme. My terror mounted as I realized the hopelessness of my plight. Nobody except Jason had reason to board this shrimp boat — nobody at all.

What about Ryan? A butterfly of hope fluttered briefly in my mind. I had promised to go to the play with Ryan tonight. Maybe he would search for me when I wasn't at Allamanda House waiting for him. But probably not. He would only think that I had stood him up. And Gram? What would she think and do? I couldn't guess. But surely Gram would instigate a search. Of course, it would be too late. Anyway, who would think of searching for me in the hold of a shrimp boat?

What to do? I refused to lie there and die without a struggle, and I knew that if I were going to help myself I would have to act before Jason came back to shoot me. What could I do? I had no idea.

With the overhead hatch closed, the hold

was like a sauna. The heat and the stink of shrimp nauseated me. I started to cry and all but choked on my sobs and the gag. Tears would get me nowhere. Slowly and painfully I managed to stand.

Leaning against the side of the boat, I began inching along as large an area as I could reach. But what did I expect to find on the side of the boat? Dropping to the floor again, I groped there, hoping to find a piece of glass, a wedge of sharp metal, or a nail. Surely there was something in the black hole that would cut through these ropes.

All I found on the floor was filth and grime. Dirt imbedded itself under my nails. My hands felt gritty. And now the shrimp stench clung to my body. Rising again, I felt along the wall once more. Suddenly I banged my head into a metal beam and almost lost consciousness. In a wild attempt to keep from falling, I whacked my hands against something sharp.

A warm, sticky fluid ran onto my fingers, and I knew I was bleeding. Although my hands were so numb that I felt no pain, I groped again for the sharp object. What was it? I couldn't be sure and I was in no mood to waste time guessing.

I found the object again. Pressing my wrist ropes against the sharp metal, I moved my hands in a sawing motion — up, down, up, down. I repeated the routine once, twice, endlessly. Perspiration ran down my face, and my smock clung to my body like a second skin. I was about to give up when I felt the ropes loosen. I worked faster, more frantically, although my wrists were rubbed raw.

After many moments my hands were loose. Shaking the ropes away, I moved my arms freely. I massaged my wrists to speed up the circulation to my numbed fingers. The gag! That was the next thing. My fingers felt like sticks, but I struggled at the knotted scarf until at last it loosened and fell around my neck. My mouth and throat were parched, but I shouted for help in spite of it. No response.

Keep calm, I thought. Jason can't get away with this. You'll find a way to escape before he returns if you'll only keep calm. Feet. Feet next, Allison.

I struggled, but no amount of effort loosened the ropes that cut into the flesh of my ankles. The sharp metal that had severed my wrist ropes was out of reach of my feet.

"Sit down and think," I said aloud. Somehow talking to myself made my situation more bearable.

To save strength, I sat and tried to figure out what to do next. I didn't realize that I had dozed until something snaked against my leg. A rat! I shrieked and began pounding the side of the boat with my hands. When I calmed down, the animal rubbed against me again. A cat!

"Kitty, kitty," I called softly as my terror subsided for a moment. "Here, kitty, kitty." What sort of a cat would be aboard a shrimp boat? A half-starved monster that might attack? Nonsense. The cat had rubbed against my ankle like an ordinary house cat. I stretched my hand into the darkness, and presently the cat rubbed against it.

"Nice kitty," I crooned. Even a cat's company was better than no company at all. For a few moments the cat was content to sit on my lap and purr, but soon it grew restless. I clutched it to my body, my mind racing.

Could the cat get off the boat? Maybe it was just prowling here for tidbits of shrimp. Or did it have a cat-sized hole somewhere — an escape hatch? Gripping the cat between my knees, I fumbled for my neck scarf and tied it to the cat's tail.

"There, kitty," I crooned. "Deliver that scarf to someone who knows me."

I released the cat, and when it was gone, I laughed bitterly at my foolishness. The cat probably couldn't get off the boat any more than I could. Even if it could, nobody at the shrimp docks would recognize my crazy scarf. Nobody except Jason. If he were still hanging around and happened to see the scarf, he would know something was up. He might come back sooner than he had planned.

Propping myself in as comfortable a position as possible, I tried to stay awake. But heat and fatigue overcame me. I dozed again. Horrible nightmares raged in my dreams. Sometime later I awakened with a start, thinking I had heard someone call my name.

Jason? I listened. I heard nothing. If it had been a dream, an hallucination, what did it matter? I was like a thirst-parched man on the desert seeing water. Only in my case I was hearing a rescuer call my name.

I was about to doze again when I snapped to attention. This time I was sure someone had called to me. Frantically I pounded on the side of the boat, shouting for help. I heard nothing except my own noise until the overhead hatch scraped across the boat deck. Stopping my racket, I gazed up into Ryan's face.

"Allison! Allison!" Ryan dropped through the hatch without bothering to use the ladder. Although I wanted to shout for joy, I broke into sobs.

"How did you know I was here?" I gasped as I became able to control myself.

"I guessed." Ryan pulled out a pocketknife and began hacking at the knots that bound my ankles. "At first I thought you had stood me up. I suppose it was my ego that wouldn't accept that answer, my ego and the memory of the other 'accidents' that have plagued you. I persuaded Bunny and Gilda to go ahead and use the theater tickets. I told them I'd wait for you and that we'd meet them later."

"But how did you happen to come to the shrimp docks?" I tried to hold still so Ryan could cut the rope without cutting me.

"You told me that you wanted to paint a shrimper," Ryan explained. "And I knew you hadn't done it yet. At least you had showed me no picture of a shrimper. When I checked in the storage closet and saw that your easel was gone, I drove over here just on a hunch."

"A good hunch," I said. "A very good hunch."

"And I stopped at the *Stella Lou* because

it was the boat that was different, the only one hoisted completely out of the water. I called your name, but you didn't answer. I was ready to leave when I saw that cat."

"The cat! My lucky scarf! It helped!"

"Right." Ryan flung the rope from my ankles and began massaging my feet to restore the circulation. "When I saw that cat prance across the deck of this boat with your scarf tied to its tail, I knew something strange was going on. Who did this to you? Jason?"

"Jason," I replied. "How dumb can I get, Ryan? You tried to warn me about him, but I wouldn't listen to you. He said he would take me sketching, but when we got here —"

"Don't talk about it anymore right now," Ryan said. "We'll deal with Jason later. Do you think you can climb that ladder and get out of here?"

"Jason was going to kill me just so he could prove that he was a better man than his father," I said, unable to stop the flow of words. "That was his reason. I accidentally got tangled up in his plans for revenge. Can you seek revenge against someone who's already dead, Ryan?"

"Let's not get technical," Ryan said. "Let's concentrate on getting out of here.

Can you make it up that ladder?"

"I can hardly move," I said. "But I have to move. Ryan, Jason's coming back with a gun. He told me so. He's going to come back here and kill me."

"Hang on to my arm," Ryan ordered. "We'll walk back and forth down here until you limber up. Duck your head or you'll bang it on something."

We walked as much as we could in the confines of the shrimp boat until at last I felt my strength and circulation returning.

"I think I can make it, Ryan. I think I can. And I'd better try. Jason may be back any minute."

"I'll go up first," Ryan said. "Don't be afraid. Stand right here and hang on to the ladder. It'll only take me a moment. When I'm at the top, I'll stretch out flat on the deck, lean through the opening, and give you a hand as I help hoist you up. Okay?"

"Okay." I trembled as Ryan turned to leave me.

But as we both looked up at the open hatch, I clutched at Ryan's arm. Jason! Overhead Jason was peering at us through the hatch, and moonlight gleamed on the blue barrel of the pistol in his right hand.

Chapter Sixteen

Instinctively I jumped back, clutching Ryan's arm and pulling him with me.

"He'll kill us both," I whispered. "He's desperate. Oh, Ryan! What have I dragged you into!"

"Come up from there," Jason called, his voice a snarl. "Come up before I climb down after you."

"Let him come down," Ryan whispered. "We have a better chance down here than up there. Maybe I can jump him."

I clung to Ryan, waiting for Jason to carry out his threat. But suddenly heavy footsteps pounding on the deck broke the terrifying silence.

"Police!" a grim voice shouted. "May we see your identification, sir?"

I strained my ears to hear.

"I work for the Ralston Shrimp Company," Jason replied smoothly. "I have permission to be aboard. I have a work pass."

"Just checking," the policeman said. "Just a routine check."

My hopes fell. The police were accepting Jason's work pass.

"You stay here," Ryan said to me. "Now's our chance. Jason's off guard."

I watched as Ryan scrambled up the ladder to the deck. "That man's armed," Ryan shouted to the policemen. "He's dangerous. He's holding a woman captive below deck. He's —"

Slowly and shakily I pulled myself up the ladder just in time to see Jason pitch his gun into the bay and make a dash for the gangplank. But Jason was too slow. Ryan tackled him, bringing him to the deck with a thud.

Jason surrendered to the police. Avoiding my gaze, he looked at his feet as he allowed the policemen to search him, handcuff him, and escort him to their patrol car.

"We'll need you two, also," one officer said to Ryan and me. "You'll have to tell your story down at headquarters."

"Could we follow you in my truck?" Ryan asked.

The officer nodded, and Ryan helped me down the gangplank, across the dock, and into his truck. As we drove to the police station, I had many questions that I wanted to ask Ryan. But I couldn't organize my thoughts well enough to phrase my queries. And maybe I didn't really need to ask questions. By this time I knew most of the answers.

Jason had been leading me on. He had been playing up to me at every opportunity so I would feel sorry for him, so I would trust him completely. And I had fallen for his line. How stupid of me not to have guessed that Jason's hatred of his father would manifest itself in some malevolent way. Why had I ignored Ryan's warning?

At the police station a matron treated my minor injuries and helped me clean myself up as best she could. Somehow I lived through the officers' questioning, and to my great relief I didn't have to face Jason again that night. When the officers dismissed Ryan and me, Ryan helped me back into his truck and we drove toward Allamanda House.

"What will happen to him?" I asked. "What do you think will happen to Jason?"

"I've no idea," Ryan said. "The law will take care of him. The thing that concerns me is what will happen to us."

"We'll have to appear in court," I said. "I'm fairly sure of that. There'll be more questions and —"

"I don't mean what will happen in our

courtroom life," Ryan said. "I mean what will happen in our personal lives?" Ryan parked the truck under a palm tree across the street from Allamanda House, leaned toward me, and kissed me. "Surely you know that I'm in love with you."

I tried to reorganize my thoughts. "Ryan! I didn't know that at all. From the moment I saw you I think I hoped that you might someday be in love with me. But I certainly didn't know. In fact I was almost — almost frightened of you."

"You hoped I might be in love with you?" Ryan asked. "You certainly never let on that those were your wishes."

"I didn't want you to think I was chasing you. And you gave me so little encouragement that I thought you disliked me for some reason. You seemed to be everybody's friend except mine. There was a barrier between us, and I wasn't the one who put it there."

"A fellow who has just been tossed aside by one girl is apt to be wary when it comes to getting involved with another girl. Surely you can understand that. Besides, I didn't want to be too quick on the rebound."

"Yes, I suppose I can understand those things," I agreed. "And I want to be truthful, Ryan. The truth is that most of the time I've known you I've been a bit frightened of you. That's why I treated you so coldly. I can't explain exactly why you frightened me. Perhaps it was the way you used your rifle that time I was aboard your fishing boat. Or maybe it was because I was sure you were following me one day at the museum. Those things made me uneasy."

"Using the rifle aboard the *Blue Dolphin* is a part of my job," Ryan replied. "A shark is too dangerous to be brought aboard a crowded boat alive. I was protecting my patrons. And as for following you, yes, I did. But I was trying to protect you from the person who was plotting against you, who pushed you into the cistern. I felt certain that all your bad luck at Allamanda House wasn't pure accident. I tried to warn you against Jason, but you wouldn't listen."

"I'm listening now," I said. "I'm listening."

"Good." Ryan smiled down at me. "While I have your full attention, I'll ask you to marry me. Now wait. Think it over, I can understand your need to paint, to see if you can make a name for yourself in the creative art world. But maybe I can find an ivory tower for two."

I thought about Jason, and I thought about Ron Baker in New York. Suddenly I realized that the reason that I hadn't wanted to get married was because up until now the right man had never asked me. But tonight the situation was different. I had never known a man like Ryan before, a man who could love me yet who didn't try to possess me, a man who could respect my need and my right to be an artist without feeling that my talent diminished him in some way.

"Gram would like to have us live at Allamanda House," I said. "I know she would. Maybe we could turn the second floor into an apartment."

"You're saying yes?"

"I'm saying yes, but I want a fairly long engagement. We have a lot of getting acquainted to do."

"I'll grant that wish," Ryan said. "But as for living at Allamanda House, no deal."

"But I thought you loved Allamanda House." I drew away from Ryan's embrace and looked into his eyes. "I thought you wanted to buy it from Gram or from Jason."

"I admire Allamanda House," Ryan said, "but it belongs to Bunny. She asked you here to help her and you've done that, Allison. There's no need to smother her with attention."

"You're right. But I'll be going to Miami tomorrow, so there's no need to worry about that."

"Right," Ryan agreed. "When we marry, we'll move to a home of our own."

I knew there was wisdom in Ryan's words. I had come here to strengthen family ties, and I would never regret having come. But sometime in the last two weeks I had matured enough to realize that the family I really longed for was one of my own. And it would begin with my marriage to Ryan.

"I may not have too much to offer you," Ryan said. "I owe thousands on the *Blue Dolphin*. A lot of my success depends on the tourist season."

"I'm not marrying you for your money," I said, pulling Ryan's head down and kissing him. "But you and the *Blue Dolphin* will do okay. Key West has seen some hard times, but I think all that is ended."

"Why do you think that?" Ryan asked.

"Because the islanders are trying to do something for others, for the visitors. No people can prosper if their success is built on another's misfortune. And that has been the story of Key West in the past. First the wrecking crews tried to prosper on the ill luck of seamen whose ships floundered on the reef. Then the cigar industry tried to thrive on the misfortunes of the Cuban workers who came here for political and financial freedom. Neither of those endeavors resulted in true success. But I believe that now that Key West people are sharing the beauty of the island, success will come and come abundantly. You're lucky to be a part of it, Ryan."

"I hope you're right," Ryan said. "I had never thought about it in just that way, but your idea makes sense."

Ryan walked with me to the door. I was glad that Gram was still at the play. There would be plenty of time later to tell her of the terrible things that had happened. Right now I wanted to be alone with my own thoughts.

And my thoughts ricocheted from Jason to Gilda to Vondetta. I couldn't help feeling sorry for Jason in spite of his attempts on my life. Jason was to be pitied. He had let hatred destroy his life. And I had long ago forgiven Gilda and Vondetta for their hostility. I couldn't help thinking of how much people are influenced by their families.

Ryan had created a good life for himself as well as a profitable business by trying to live up to his father's image. On the other hand, Jason had destroyed himself by seeking revenge, by trying to be better than his father. Generations of family resentment had influenced Gilda's life, and Vondetta had been weakened by a marriage that had failed.

I thought about myself. Hadn't my lack of family ties been the thing that had brought me to Key West? Perhaps every couple who ever married influenced generations to come. It was a sobering thought. But as I sat there waiting for Gram to return, I knew that my experiences at Allamanda House had strengthened me to face whatever lay ahead.

We hope you have enjoyed this Large Print book. Other Thorndike Press or Chivers Press Large Print books are available at your library or directly from the publishers.

For more information about current and upcoming titles, please call or write, without obligation, to:

Publisher
Thorndike Press
295 Kennedy Memorial Drive
Waterville, ME   04901
Tel. (800) 223-1244
Tel. (800) 223-6121

OR

Chivers Press Limited
Windsor Bridge Road
Bath BA2 3AX
England
Tel. (0225) 335336

All our Large Print titles are designed for easy reading, and all our books are made to last.